GUARDIAN'S SHADOW

Fire and Snow
Book Three

KHLOE WREN

Books by Khloe Wren

Fire and Snow:
Guardian's Heart
Noble Guardian
Guardian's Shadow
Fierce Guardian (due out mid '16)

Dragon Warriors:
Enchanting Eilagh
Binding Becky
Claiming Carina
Seducing Skye
Believing Binda

Single Titles:
Fireworks
Jaguar Secrets
Tigers Are Forever
Bad Alpha Anthology
Scarred Perfection
Scandals: Zeck

ISBN: 978-0-9945190-5-4

Cover Credits:
Photographer: Billy Dee Williams of Ab Salute Fotog LLC
Model: Dustin Rhoads
Digital Artist: Jay Aheer of Simply Defined Art

Editing Credits:
Editor: Carolyn Depew of Write Right
Proofreader: Ami Deason

Acknowledgements

As with every book I write, I couldn't have done it without my beautiful and infinitely patient husband. He not only keeps the house running when I get lost in book world but he helps me thrash out plot issues too! Truly, he is my hero. To my girls, thank you for sharing Mummy with the world inside her head. To my parents, your continual unconditional love and support means the world to me.

I cannot thank my gorgeous critique partner enough. Tamsin Baker, you are a wonderful friend and an awesome critiquer. You never fail to call me on my crap and this book is so much better for it. To my divine beta-readers, Abee, Lyn and Christine. Thank you for helping round off the rough edges. To rally driver, Brendan Reeves. Thank you for allowing me to interview you and helping me get the rallying parts of the book accurate. Abee Eduards and Gabriela Rivera, thank you for all your help with Chilean information and phrases.

To all my friends, especially those in Four Angels and the Naughty Book Club. Your words of support and advice have kept me going. To my editing team, I thank you for putting up with the nightmares my bad gives give you to help me make this book all it could be.

And finally, those involved in my cover art. Billy, I gave you the description and you found Dustin for me, the perfect model for Jessie. Jay, your artistry skills have blown me away once more.

xo
Khloe

Biography

Khloe Wren grew up in the Adelaide Hills before her parents moved the family to country South Australia when she was a teen. It was there that Khloe followed her father's footsteps and joined the volunteer firefighting service at 18. A few years later, Khloe moved to Melbourne which unfortunately meant she had to give up firefighting but she's always missed it. After a few years living in the big city, she missed the fresh air and space of country living so returned to rural South Australia. Khloe currently lives in the Murraylands with her incredibly patient husband, two strong willed young daughters, an energetic dog and two curious cats.

Khloe has always loved big cats, especially Snow Leopards. So it seemed only natural that when she began writing her first novel after having major surgery that left her on bedrest for six months, that she chose these beautiful creatures as her first shifters.

Glossary

Alpha (of a Leap): The leader of the Leap.

Continental Leap: The Leap chosen to represent their continent at the Council of Alphas. Each of the seven continents has a Continental Leap.

Council of Alphas: The Alpha of each Continental Leap form the Council of Alphas. It is their job to oversee all aspects of shifter life.

Dream Bonding: After the female turns twenty-one, shifter pairs can pull each other into a dream. Useful for when mates are apart from each other.

Chaton: French for kitten.

Comet Shifters: Those shifters newly created from Halley's Comet's passing of Earth.

David Jones: Large department store.

Firie/Firies/Firie's: Nickname for a firefighter

Halley's Comet: When the shifters were first created. Halley's Comet passed as the magic was welded. Now, every seventy-five years when the comet passes over Earth, a new pair of shifters is conceived on each continent.

Jaws of Life: Apparatus Firefighters use to cut open crashed vehicles in order to save the occupants

Leap: Leap is the name given to a group of Snow Leopards.

Lost Ones: Shifters who are not part of a Leap and often don't know of their heritage. Lost Ones are often alone and scared of what they are, not understanding there are others like them.

Maman: French for Mum/Mom

Marking, The: After mating, the couple mark each other with permanent scratch marks to show their claim on the other. The mark looks like four wide scratch marks that reveal Snow Leopard spots beneath.

Mating: The process a couple goes through to bind themselves together for life. Mating forms an unbreakable bond.

Ma chère: French endearment, my dear.

Mon amour: French endearment, my love.

Petit fille: French for little girl/daughter

Search, The: On of the Council of Alphas' main purposes is to go looking for Lost Ones and Comet Shifters.

Shifter Magic: Because shifters were created with magic, they hold a low level of magic which they can weld on occasion.

Tibetan Monks: Tibetan Monks are the ones who originally cast the magic to bind a man and a Snow Leopard together.

Trigger: Trigger Corporation is the enemy to the shifters.

Ute: Similar to an American Pickup Truck

Widow Mate: Mate of a shifter who has died. Once their mate dies, they are free to find love again if they choose to.

Dedication

For Kira:

Kit was always going to be for you.

Chapter One

The air around Jessie buzzed with excitement and anticipation. Just like most of the people here, Jessie was on a high even though he'd already been in Tasmania, Australia, for five days. It was October, which meant it was time for the annual International Bethotte Rally. The rally hadn't officially started yet, but with all the teams needing to do reconnaissance of the track before they began racing, the hospitality tent was full of people tonight. Along with his co-driver and longtime friend, Pedro Huxley, Jessie was finishing his meal when his gaze caught sight of her. Instantly all other thoughts left his mind.

Just like in his dreams, she was stunning. Tall for a woman, at around six feet, her flame-red hair made her stand out in the crowd. She stood near the tent's entry with her hands on her hips, which kept her yellow firefighter's jacket open to reveal a tight navy muscle shirt with 'FIRE' written across the front beneath her uniform's red suspenders. His pulse went up as he took in the curves of her breasts beneath the tight fabric.

"You all right there, *amigo*?"

Pedro gripped his shoulder and gave him a little shake. Jessie gulped in air to ease his burning lungs, making him realize he'd been holding his breath.

"It's her."

"Her? Your dream girl? The one that's been haunting your nights for what, four years now? This I have to see. Where is she?"

After having way too much to drink one night, Jessie had confessed to Pedro about his nightly fantasies. Ever since his twenty-first birthday, Jessie had dreamed of the same woman every single night. The female wasn't the only thing that remained the same, the location did as well. Each time Jessie found himself in a small clearing within a dark forest where he was forced into a state of helplessness, unable to move or speak at all.

At the beginning, it had been just glimpses of her face, but each dream revealed a little more of her until he knew what every inch of her clothed form looked like. His dream girl wasn't frozen like he was in the dreams. She was always free to move and speak as she wished. Lately, that meant she stalked around him wearing a tight black t-shirt, fitted jeans and bright red Doc Martin boots. The woman's emotions were intense. Some nights she would rage at him for not having come for her yet, on others she'd cry as though she was in agony. Those nights were the worst. He would feel her pain straight through his heart, as if he'd been shot, and it would last beyond the night. He'd had days where he could barely function due to his distraction with his dream girl.

"The red-haired firefighter over there."

Pedro whistled softly, "*Hermosa*, she's dream worthy. Pretty sure she's going to feature in a couple of mine now I've seen her."

A possessive rage descended over him and he thumped his friend in the arm. "Eyes to yourself. She's mine, and mine alone."

Jessie shook his head to clear it. Did he just growl at Pedro?

"Whoa, Jessie. I'm just talking shit. You know me. This isn't like you, *amigo*. You think it's got something to do with your, ah, feline tendencies?"

Aside from his parents, Pedro was the only person Jessie had trusted with his secret. How, on his fifteenth birthday, as the moon rose, he'd changed into a snow leopard. He'd been scared out of his mind by the time his parents had found him hours later. His father had accused his mother of cheating on him. The bastard claimed there was no way his genetics could have produced such a monster. His mama vowed she'd always been faithful. That had started his father on a rant about black magic.

From that moment on, Jessie had always been very careful to keep his secret safe. He'd only told Pedro after five years of friendship. He needed someone to talk to about it all and had prayed his friend wouldn't reject him. Jessie shouldn't have worried. Pedro had just slapped him on the back and made some smart-ass comment about how he now knew why Jessie's reflexes were so good.

"No fucking idea, Pedro. I mean, surely I'm not the only one like it on the damn planet?"

"Can't tell you, *amigo*. But we did find those stories about snow leopards being seen in the Cradle Mountains National Park. That's not far from here. Maybe there's some truth to them and she's like you. Are you going to go over to her? Because, *amigo*, she's seen you staring."

Jessie tensed as he focused on her eyes. He'd been looking at her without really seeing her while he was lost in thought. Now he was under the intense scrutiny of her green gaze. Like the rest of her, they were exquisite. Slightly slanted and framed by thick lashes. Together with her olive skin tone, he'd guess she was South American, not Australian.

"I suppose now she's caught me staring I should at least go say hi. You coming, right?"

"Of course, Jessie. I'll always have your back, on and off the track."

That made Jessie grin. Damn but the two of them had been in some sticky situations over the years. Rally drivers liked adrenaline, and on the track that was great. Off of it? It got them into trouble more often than not.

"I know, *amigo*."

They headed over to the small group of firefighters who were still standing near the entry to the tent. As they walked closer, Jessie's palms began to sweat. He had no idea what to say to her. He'd never had trouble talking to women before. His reputation of being able to pick up women no matter what country they were in, proved that. Pedro joked it was his *animal magnetism* that women couldn't resist.

His dream girl stopped talking and tilted her head to the side as she frowned at his approach. The four men standing near her glanced between them with bewildered expressions. *Whatever*. He was here for her.

"*Hola*, I'm Jessie Lutrec. One of the drivers. What's your name, *reinita*?"

"Hey. The name's Kit."

Jessie sucked in a breath as his body all but vibrated from hearing her real voice, close to how he'd dreamed of it, only better. As if his dreams were a muted version of the real woman. He raised his hand to shake her outstretched palm, just making contact when it all went to hell.

"Yo, Lutrec! You moving up from the groupies to the firies this year, huh? Gonna leave nothing for the rest of us, the way you're going."

Kit stood silent, her mouth gaping a little as the four men with her all moved forward at once, blocking her from his view. With a frustrated growl, he spun and marched over to the idiot who'd spoken.

"Hacket, would have thought by the third broken nose, you'd know when to keep your *puta boco* shut."

Jessie was out for blood. Sparks continued to buzz through his system from the brief touch he'd shared with Kit. As he approached Hacket, the man's sole brain cell apparently came on line.

"Whoa, buddy. Lutrec, I was just messing with ya. You know, having some fun?"

"We have never been buddies, Hacket."

He went to reach for the bastard when suddenly Pedro was in his face.

"Step back, Jessie. You fight now, you'll be booted off this event. And honestly, Hacket is not worth the trouble. Come on, *amigo*. Take a couple of deep breaths and calm down."

Pedro tapped a finger near his eye. Damn it, he was overreacting if his eye was twitching. Jessie rolled his shoulders as he backed up and turned to leave the tent. He needed some time alone to cool off and attempt to reconcile the fact his dream girl was not a figment of his imagination as he'd always thought.

Kit stared down at her hand in shock. Was that playboy rally driver her mate? They'd barely touched before she gained four bodyguards that proceeded to block her from him. But she could still feel the sparks shooting around her blood stream. Even though Kit couldn't see him anymore, she had no trouble hearing him cursing the other driver who'd insulted him. She pushed between Joel and Nick to see what would happen next. She really hoped her mate wasn't going to be a total hot head that brawled at every opportunity.

"Racing hasn't even started yet and we got asshole drivers to deal with. Kit, you sure you want to do this?"

"Joel, you know full well I can more than handle myself, along with any drivers who think I'm on the bloody menu."

"So why didn't you plant that Lutrec bloke on his ass? Normally our job is pulling you off assholes, not protecting you from them."

She clenched and released her hand a few times in an attempt to ease the tingling sensation still running over her flesh as Jessie stormed from the tent without having thrown a punch.

"Because it would seem that particular asshole is mine."

"Holy shit! He's your mate? Where the hell is he going then?"

Kit pushed past her leap brothers to head out of the tent. She'd kept her past close to her chest all these years. Even as a teenager, she hadn't wanted to be treated differently. But she knew, once word got out she was a comet shifter, things would change. She'd be labeled as different and would be rejected. Well, she knew Jake and Sophie wouldn't do that, because they already knew. They also knew her greatest fear was to lose this new family she'd gained. They'd told her so many times that it wouldn't change how the leap saw her, but she couldn't trust it. Not after what her own flesh and blood had done.

Blinking back tears along with memories that were surging to the surface, Kit raced to her hotel room. Being the only female firefighter had its benefits, one of which was her own room. Her fingers shook as she attempted to unlock the door. On the third try the card slid into the slot and finally, the little green light signaled her success. She shoved her way into the darkness and leaned against the closed door. Memories surged to the surface of her consciousness and sweat broke out over her body as they broke free of the tight rein she kept on them. On a sob, she slid down until her bottom hit the floor. Burying her face in her hands, she silently cried as her mind began replaying that horrific night when her world came crashing down.

"Melina, it's past your bedtime."

"But, Mama, I'm too old for a bedtime!"

"You have school in the morning, and so long as you have to get up early, you need to go to bed early. That's just life so deal with it. Off you go."

Frustrated that her parents wouldn't treat her like the young lady she now was, she stomped off to bed. She was going to be fifteen tomorrow. Then on Saturday she was having a quinceanera; *a big party with her whole class coming. Maybe she'd even be able to convince Donny to kiss her for her birthday...*

Hours later she woke feeling ill. Her body shivered and she was covered in sweat. Her mind felt foggy as she glanced at her bedside cupboard. Two forty-five in the morning. Why the hell was she awake now? And what did she eat that made her feel like this? Her body felt as if it was on fire. She stumbled from her bed and landed hard on the floor as she began panting for breath. She looked out her open curtains to see a sliver of the moon rising over the horizon as her vision filled with blue light.

When her mind cleared, she felt different. She opened her eyes and saw she had paws. What the fuck? She tried to walk over to her dresser, but stumbled and tripped over herself. Eventually she got there and looked up into the glass. She was a damn cat! White and grey with spots. A snow leopard maybe? Her heart was racing and her mind was a complete mess as she tried to process what was happening.

Her bedroom door banged open and her father entered with his fists raised ready to fight.

"Melina? You okay-"

He froze when he saw her. She tried to speak but it came out as a strange meowing noise. Why couldn't she be human? She didn't want to be a cat. She closed her eyes as she sobbed, and a tingle ran through her body. She held her breath as she opened her eyes and found she was human again.

"Oh phew. I'm back."

Relief flooded her system as she looked down at her naked body. She looked to her doorway to see both her parents staring at her.

"What are you?"

"I don't know, Papa. But I'm still me, Melina."

He shook his head at her. "You are not my daughter. Get out of my house and never let me see you again."

Kit fell to her side as the sobs wracked her body. That had been the last time she'd seen her parents. The last time someone had called her 'Melina'. Eleven years ago next month. How could it still hurt so much?

Kit forced herself to move, and to strip out of her clothes. Once naked, she gave in to her instincts and shifted to her leopard form. The animal was now familiar to her. She loved being in this form. She felt free and her senses were heightened. With a low growl, she cursed the rally and the fact she was stuck in a hotel room when she wanted to go for a run. If she were home, she'd head up to the mountains and run till her lungs burned. After stalking around the small room for a while, she sighed before she reluctantly shifted back. Feeling calmer, she entered the bathroom to shower and attempt to put her mental walls back in place. She had a feeling she was going to need all her strength to deal with her mate.

Half an hour later, Kit lay awake in bed. Her mind and instincts were wired—too much so for her to relax enough to sleep. She glanced at the clock. Nine at night. Not too late. Sophie should still be awake. Grabbing her mobile, Kit sent her leap mother a text.

"You awake? Really need to talk."

"Getting late for text messages. Are you expecting any trouble?"

"No, not sure who it would be."

Sophie grabbed her phone from the coffee table before returning to sit by her husband's side. His arm wrapped around her shoulder as he laid a gentle kiss to the top of her head. She smiled as she breathed in his masculine scent. After all these years, Jake was still everything she ever wanted or needed.

She hummed in pleasure as she swiped her screen to unlock the phone.

"It's Kit. She's working the rally isn't she? Wonder what's happened."

"Yeah, she's up there with Nick, Joel, Jordan and Beau this year. What's she want at this time of night?"

Sophie smiled a little as she read the text. Kit knew Sophie detested modern text-slang and always took the time to write out all the words in full.

"She's asking if I'm still up, says she needs to talk. It's been a long time since she's reached out like this, especially so late at night."

Sophie frowned as her maternal instincts flared. Something was wrong. Kit may not biologically be hers, but after rescuing her when she was a teen, Sophie had gladly taken the young woman in and treated her as though she'd birthed her. As she pressed the dial button, and held the phone to her ear in such a way that Jake would be able to hear, she thought back to those early days when they'd first brought Kit home to Rosebery. Kit had clung to Sophie to begin with, desperate for love and acceptance. However, it hadn't taken long for her to find her inner strength, and now Kit had grown into a very strong, independent woman who rarely needed to lean on her leap mother—or anyone else for that matter.

"Hey, Soph. Thanks for calling so fast."

"No problem, kitten. You know I'm always here for you. So, what's been happening? Those hot shot rally drivers giving you grief?"

"Nah, you know me, it's nothing I can't handle."

The hairs on Sophie's neck stood up at the strained tone her girl was using, and the fact Kit didn't tell her off for using the nickname they'd first used with her when they found her. Normally, she was quick to tell them that she was far from a kitten.

"So, what's tugging at your tail then?"

"My mate."

Jake stiffened behind her as Sophie sucked in a shocked breath.

"Finally. He's found you."

"Not on purpose, he didn't. Oh, Soph. What do I do? He looked totally shocked to see me. Then another driver trash talked him, and the boys heard and became instant bodyguards. He just stormed off. Didn't even look back."

Jake leaned down to whisper in her ear, "Ask for his name. I'm going to find him tomorrow and help fix this."

She smiled as she glanced up at her mate, her alpha. Always there for their leap.

"You know your leap brothers will always have your back, Kit. They didn't do anything to him did they? And, Kit? Does this mystery man have a name?"

She chuckled a little at that, "His name is Jessie Lutrec. A playboy rally driver from Chile. And no, the boys didn't overstep with him. They didn't need to." Kit's heavy sigh came through the line.

"Are you sure you want to work the rally this year? You sound worn out and it hasn't even officially started yet. I know you're still worried over the situation with Tina."

"Yeah, but Tina's safe now that she's with Conner and living at your place, and if I stayed I would have gone looking for that bitch Robyn myself. And as much as the woman has it coming, I don't want to risk ending up in the system for taking her down."

Kit had never explained her reasons for wanting to keep such a low profile, and Sophie and Jake had let her have her secrets. The situation with their youngest son wasn't good. His wheelchair-bound mate had been left in a burning house by the woman hired to care for her, Robyn, and Conner had been hurt saving her from the flames. They were thankfully both all right now and living with her and Jake. But Robyn was still at large.

"Tina's father has arrived now. So hopefully it will all be cleared up soon with Tina safe and with Conner."

"I hope so. I like her. She hasn't deserved the shit she's copped."

"Much like you, Kit. Neither of you have deserved any of the pain you've been dealt. I suspect Jessie has had his fair share of rejection and hurt too. I wonder if he's ever met another shifter? You know he's been dreaming of you for the past four years now, quite probably with no idea why. Seeing you today, realizing you're real and not simply a figment of his imagination would have been quite the shock."

Kit didn't respond straight away and Sophie's muscles tightened. Had she said the wrong thing and put Kit off side?

"Still think that's totally unfair. Why can't the women dream of their mates? I would have tracked him down years ago, if I'd only known what he looked like."

She smiled as pride for her girl filled her. "Yet you tried to find him. Don't think for a moment Jake and I didn't know what those trips were about a few years back. You were searching Chile weren't you?"

Kit chuckled a little. "Yeah. I knew he'd be in South America. Since I was born in Chile, I assumed he'd be there. Damn, I was so naive. I thought if I simply walked around for long enough, he would see me and come get me. The two trips just confirmed that my leap family here in Tasmania is my home and life. I got so homesick on both trips, Soph. That's why I didn't go a third time."

"You know, now you've seen Jessie, you can pull him into a bond-dream?"

"Really? I thought the male had to at least start things off."

"Adele pulled Dominic into a dream to tell him she was moving to Tasmania. Not many women initiate them. They don't normally have to. But I doubt Jessie knows about mates, Kit. I suspect he's currently more confused than you are about today. He's a lost one, kitten. Don't be too hard on the man just yet. You remember what it was like before Jake and I found you?"

"Yeah, it was horrific. Thinking I was some kind of freak that no one would ever want."

"Jessie's probably been feeling like that for the best

part of the past ten years. Now he's been identified, he won't be alone anymore. Jake will contact him tomorrow and start educating him on what he is and his heritage. We'll help you both every step of the way, Kit."

"The whole leap will know."

The crack in Kit's voice brought tears to Sophie's eyes. She could understand Kit's fear of rejection but it was so unnecessary and heartbreaking.

"Kit, your parents were wrong to reject you like they did. Your leap family will not do the same thing when they discover you're a comet shifter. Why don't you mention it to the twins as a test? I dare say all the boys up there will work it out soon enough if Jessie doesn't start chasing your tail every chance he gets."

"But what if you're wrong? What if it does change how they treat me?"

Sophie wanted to reach through the phone and give Kit a shake. Had she forgotten how strong she was? That she wasn't that lost girl anymore?

"If any of those boys give you any grief, you'll do what you've always done, Kit. You'll put them on their asses. Are you forgetting who you are, Kit? I guarantee they haven't. You have never taken crap from anybody, and have always been there to defend anyone else who's copping any. We are all extra grateful for the protection you've provided to both Tina and Kelly in particular this last year. But that's just two of many you've helped. If finding out about your conception changes their opinion of you, it will be because they'll respect you all the more for what you've survived. No one aside from Jake and I know anything about you from before you came to live with us. Hell, you haven't even shared your birth name with anyone, including us!"

"I wish I could believe you, Soph. I really do. Although, you are right about me forgetting who I am. I'm not that lost teenager anymore. I'm strong and I will kick the ass of anyone who tries to make me feel like that little girl again." She paused for a deep breath. "Thank you, Soph. I think I'm calm enough now that I can get some sleep. I'll have a shot at pulling Jessie into a dream, and if Jake could talk to him as soon as he's able, that would great."

"Jake will track him down in the morning, Kit. He won't waste time on this. Good night, Kit. Sweet dreams, kitten."

"Night, Soph. Thanks again."

After returning her phone to the coffee table, Sophie climbed into Jake's lap. She needed to feel his comfort.

"Tell me they're going to be okay."

"They'll be fine, my love. I'll find Jessie, and bring him into the fold. And you know Kit, she won't let Jessie disappear on her."

He had a point there. Kit had grown into such a strong woman—both inside and out. Sophie took her husband's face in her palms and kissed him, losing herself to her man's warm embrace. All her worries melted away as he took control with a low growl. When they broke apart, they were both panting.

"I love you, Jake White. Even after all these years, you are still my center. Take me to bed, love. I need to feel you inside me."

She watched Jake's eyes glaze over with arousal.

"Ah, Soph, what you do to me... I love you so much, my sweet alpha mate and, as always, your wish is my command."

Contentment and liquid fire coursed through Sophie's veins as her husband carried her to their bedroom.

"Just think, once we have Conner and Tina sorted, we'll have the whole place to ourselves once again. No more having to wait until we get to the bedroom."

Sophie playfully thumped his chest as she giggled moments before he laid her down on their bed and covered her body with his.

"You're going to wear a hole in the carpet if you keep up your pacing, *amigo*."

Jessie stopped to glare at this friend as he spoke to him in their native South American Spanish. In public, they always spoke English, but in private, no matter what country they were in, they stuck with the familiar. Normally, it helped Jessie center himself. But not tonight.

"Like I care if I wear out the hotel's floor. I need to think, so I need to move."

What he really wanted to do was shift and go for a run. But he couldn't. It was too risky in this unfamiliar place. Last thing he needed was to be caught and put in a zoo or something worse.

"Pedro, do you think she's like me?"

"A shifter? I guess she could be. That would explain why you've been dreaming about her."

"Doubt I'll get to even talk to her now. Not after Hacket shot his mouth off. Those four big firemen didn't look happy with me."

"Jessie, she would have found out about your reputation soon enough even if Hacket hadn't spoken. You've never tried to keep your luck with the ladies quiet."

"Yeah, yeah. I know."

"Try to forget about her for the moment. We have one more day of recce, then two days of registration. Wait until the welcoming party. You should be able to catch her attention there."

Recce was slang for reconnaissance, which would need all his focus, but the days of registration were boring and he didn't need to be alert. Jessie scrubbed his face with his palms. Three days. He could wait that long. By then he'd have his thoughts in some sort of order, and would be able to ask her some questions. The way she'd gasped when their skin touched proved she'd felt something at the connection, and she hadn't looked frightened by it either. Only shocked.

"Right. Three days. I can do that. I'm going to hit the bathroom, then call it a night."

"Dare say I'll be snoring before you come back out. Night, Jessie."

"Night, Pedro."

Twenty minutes later, fresh from the shower, Jessie climbed into his bed, chuckling at the quiet snore coming from Pedro. Every night the man would fall asleep within minutes of laying down. Jessie was the same way most evenings. Fortunately, noises didn't bother him, especially low sounds like his friend was currently making.

Rolling onto his side, he glanced out the window at the shrubbery surrounding the hotel. It all looked so peaceful...

Jessie found himself back in the hospitality tent, except this time, aside from Kit, it was empty of people.

"Well, this is different."

"I was wondering if you were going to sleep at all tonight."

He lowered his head on a sigh; it might be a new location, but apparently the dialog was going to be the same as always.

"Just what I need. Another night filled with dreams of you screaming at me."

"Excuse me?"

Jessie's head snapped up in shock. She'd never heard him before.

"You can hear me?"

"Of course I can, Jessie. Why on earth wouldn't I?"

"Because in the four years I've been dreaming of you, you've never once answered any of my questions."

"Well, I guess that's part of the mate dreams you boys

have. This is different. This is a bond dream."

Jessie didn't think you were meant to be able to get a headache in a dream, but he was rapidly proving that theory wrong.

"I have no idea what you're talking about, Kit."

She crossed her arms over her delicious looking breasts as she regarded him with a small smile.

"You've never met another shifter before have you?"

Jessie frowned at her as he rested his hands on his hips.

"What do you know about shifters?"

Jessie stumbled back in shock as Kit was suddenly engulfed in a ball of blue light. Before his vision fully cleared, he felt soft fur rub against his legs.

"Conche tu madre!"

Dazed, he watched the sleek snow leopard walk away before it returned to being Kit.

"You are not the only one, Jessie. Far from it."

"How did you not lose your clothes when you shifted?"

"Because this is a dream. In the real world, we can't do it without shredding whatever we're wearing. Most of us keep at least one change of clothes in our vehicle."

"We? Us? How many are there?"

"Worldwide? Thousands. Here in Rosebery, we'd be getting close to one hundred, I think. You'll be getting a call or a visit from our alpha tomorrow. His name is Jake White. He'll help you, teach you everything you need to know."

Jessie dropped down into a chair as he rubbed the bridge of his nose.

"How is this even possible? I'm dreaming, yet you're telling me things I don't know—and I know my imagination isn't this good."

"It's not. This is a bond dream. You and I are very much real and we'll both remember what happens here. It is still a dream in that where we are, isn't real, and any injuries we sustain while here won't carry over to the real world."

"So, you make a habit of invading men's dreams do you?"

Kit huffed and glared at him before she paced away from him. She turned and stormed right up to him, her gaze pure fury as she gripped a fist in his shirt and lifted him from his seat. Suddenly his chair vanished and a cold brick wall appeared at his back.

"Listen up, boy. *Dream bonding only ever happens between mates. Every shifter has only one. On the female's twenty-first birthday, the male will begin to dream of her. It's then up to him to find his mate. I've been waiting for a bloody long time for you to get off your ass and come looking. I am not in the mood to listen to you call me a slut. I am not the one known the world over as a playboy. I've stupidly been waiting for you, while you have been hooking up with any woman dumb enough to spread her thighs!"*

Jessie's mind spun. His mouth was dry and he couldn't find his voice. He had a mate? And she was a virgin?

This woman, his dream girl, was his fated mate? And what the hell did 'mate' mean exactly?

Kit thumped him against the wall with a growl, "And now you have nothing to say? I know you feel the bond between us. The connection. Apparently, you just aren't man enough to do anything about it."

Never had Jessie seen a woman so furious. In stunned silence he fell to the floor when Kit released his shirt and stalked away to fade from the dream.

He closed his eyes and leaned back against the wall. Somehow his entire world just got upended and he wasn't so sure he liked the changes. He couldn't help but chuckle as the old adage be careful what you wish for *ran through his mind. All he'd ever wanted was to find other shifters. Find out why he was what he was. He hoped this guy, Jake, had some answers for him, because he really didn't want to have to try and get Kit to tell him anything for a while. That woman needed some time to cool off before seeing him again.*

Chapter Two

Jake nervously rubbed the back of his neck as he sat with Dominic at a small cafe on the outskirts of Launceston waiting for Jessie. His heightened empathy always made these initial meetings difficult. Lost ones like Jessie, who'd never met other shifters before, felt plenty of strong emotions. Even if they knew his issue and tried to curb their feelings, it would still be a battle for Jake to not be sick from the overload.

"So, Jessie is a comet shifter. That means Kit is one too, right?"

Grateful for the reprieve from his thoughts, Jake smiled at his son, their leap's next alpha.

"That's correct. They are the South American pair. Your mother and I kept it quiet because Kit didn't want anyone to know. Do you remember when we first brought Kit home?"

"Kind of. You were gone for what? Two, three weeks? Then you both returned, along with a very timid, frightened Kit. Any questions we had about her received the same answers 'it's not for you to know' or 'she'll tell you when she's ready'."

"That still holds true, but as future alpha you will need

to know things that the rest of the leap does not. This includes very personal details that you must keep to yourself—what I tell you today you cannot even discuss with Kit, unless of course, she brings it up."

Dominic frowned. "I understand not talking to everyone else—but why not Kit?"

"Because, son, beneath the tough exterior Kit shows the world, she is that scared teenager who fears rejection."

Dominic's shock and hurt rippled through him. He hid the wince as Dominic again spoke.

"Rejection? From me? Nothing she could do or say would change how I feel. She's my sister."

Pride for his eldest son bloomed within his heart and for the moment, it pushed all the other emotions he was absorbing out of his body.

"I've been telling her that for years, Dominic. But she's scared. The morning after her first shift, her parents kicked her out. It was three weeks after her birthday when Choden led us to her. She was starved, barely alive and in leopard form. She has never confided in me all that took place in those three weeks. I do know she first tried to live on the streets of Sydney in her human form, and that she struggled to the point she gave up and decided to live as an animal. Of course, with no training or skills she couldn't hunt very well. I don't know why she stuck to her leopard form until the point of being near death. Not sure if she'll ever trust anyone enough to tell-"

"Better leave it there, Dad. Looks like our newest

recruit is here."

Jake followed his son's gaze and watched as a tall young man with short light brown hair walked up to them. Jake stood to shake the man's hand.

"Jessie Lutrec?"

"Yes. I assume you're Jake."

He nodded. "And this is my son Dominic. Take a seat. Would you like a coffee?"

"Ah, yeah. Coffee would be great."

Dominic rose to stand. "I'll go grab it for you. How do you take it?"

"Flat white, one sugar. Thanks."

Waves of doubt and anxiety mixed with hope poured from Jessie, all emotions Jake had expected to feel from the man. Jake struggled to keep composed as he took his time sitting back down. He took a few calming breaths to make sure his voice would be level before he spoke.

"So, recce went well? Think your car is up to the task?"

Jessie's face lit up and he visibly relaxed. His joy and passion for rallying were a balm to Jake. Thankfully, his empathic senses picked up the good and the bad. Jake kept the conversation light until Dominic returned, enjoying the reprieve of negative emotions while he could.

"Well, I know you have limited time before you need to be back, so tell me, what do you want to know first?"

"How were shifters created? Why me? I mean, I was a completely normal kid until my fifteenth birthday, then bam. I'm suddenly part animal. I know neither of my parents can shift form."

Jake clenched his jaw. Not only had Jessie's eyes darkened as he said that last part, but fury and agony radiated from him. Like smog, the emotions attempted to smother Jake. Days like today he wished he wasn't one of the few shifters who had an enhanced skill. After so many years of practice, he managed to push the emotions aside so he could think clearly again. He wondered if Jessie and Kit's shared pain would make them a stronger couple in the long run. Mentally shaking his head, Jake focused back on Jessie's question.

"I think it best I start from the beginning, with the creation of the very first shifter. Back in 1759, high in the Tibetan mountains, there was a Buddhist monastery. It's still there actually. Anyway, this group of monks spent a lot of time with a local leap of snow leopards.

"When a large number of leopards started disappearing, they became concerned. The animals couldn't keep themselves safe from human hunters and poachers. An elder monk, along with his young prodigy, began researching all manner of things, trying to find a way to prevent the leopards from becoming extinct. Eventually, they found a spell. It was designed to combine a man with an animal. They thought by joining a human with a snow leopard, it would give them the ability to protect the animals from other humans that wanted to do them harm.

"The elder monk was near the end of his life, so his

young prodigy, Choden, offered to participate in the joining. Choden had a particularly close bond with a young snow leopard already, so it made sense to choose him. Now, this spell they found needed nature-based power, so they performed it at night as the full moon rose."

As Jake had spoken, Jessie had moved to lean forward and Jake was happy to see the man was still listening intently. The steady ripple of emotion now contained anticipation and curiosity, feelings Jake had a much easier time absorbing without repercussions.

"So that's why I shifted that first time in the middle of the night? Because the moon didn't rise until then?"

Jake liked that Jessie wasn't just listening but thinking things through. With his quick mind, Jessie would be an asset to their leap, that was for sure.

"Yes, that's right. Choden was fifteen years old when the spell was cast. So as the moon rises on a shifter's fifteenth birthday, they shift for the first time. But the moon wasn't the only thing that gave its power to the spell. Unbeknown to the monks, Halley's Comet was passing over the Earth that night. The magic was boosted by the comet's strength and it became tied into the spell. So when Choden was changed into a shifter, the added power caused a pair of shifters to be conceived on each continent as well. Each of the pairs went on to pass the shifter DNA on to their children when they had them. That's how most shifters are now created; they are born to at least one shifter parent."

"But neither of my parents are shifters. My father attempted to tell me my mother must have cheated on him with another man, but she swears she's never strayed from him. And I look too much like him for him to not be my biological father."

With a wince Jake again pushed aside Jessie's emotions. Anger and guilt this time. Jake wasn't sure what the guilt was about but he'd worry about it another time.

"I said that's how *most* are created. Not all. Every seventy-five years, Halley's Comet passes back over the Earth. When it does, another pair is conceived on each continent. You and Kit were conceived on its last passing in 1986. You are the South American Comet Shifter Pair."

Jake rubbed at his temples and paused to take a few mouthfuls of his coffee. Jessie's emotions were all over the place now. Relief, confusion, hurt…they were melding together into a storm of feelings that were going to make Jake physically ill soon, but he'd do his best to finish this session with Jessie. Poor kid had enough to worry about without trying to tamp down his reactions on Jake's behalf.

"So Kit was telling the truth? The reason I've dreamed of her is because we're *mates*."

"Ahh, so Kit went ahead with dream bonding last night. Dreams are important between mates. On the female's twenty-first birthday, the male begins to dream of her. As you know, it's just flashes at first, then as time progresses you get shown more. The idea behind it is that you look for her, the longer it takes, the more information you get to help you find her. Of course, you had no idea why you were dreaming of her. I don't doubt you received quite a shock when you saw she was a real person."

Jessie chuckled without humor. "Yeah, you could say that. What's the go with dream bonding?"

"Mates can pull each other into a dream. Not every shifter will do it. A lot of shifters believe it's invading their mate's privacy and refuse to do it, at least until after they have met."

Dominic sat forward. "May I explain?"

He nodded to his son. "Yes, I believe you will do better than I with this side of things, as you were forced to rely on them for a time."

Jake had also used it to find his own mate, but Dominic would be better for Jessie. They were similar in age and honestly, Jake needed a few minutes to deal with the emotions he'd absorbed without having to concentrate on talking calmly.

"Jessie, when I started dreaming of Adele, my human mate, she was in a lot of emotional pain. I could feel it through our bond. It felt like a claw in my heart. I had to know if she was injured. At that point, I had no idea where she was. To be honest, I'd forgotten about the dream bonding. As Dad said, it's not used all that much. But when he suggested it to me, I knew it was the best way to find out what was going on. So I pulled Adele into a dream. My first attempt was as a human man and she refused to give me any attention. So I tried again as a snow leopard. That worked. As a leopard, she confided in me how her mother was dying of cancer and that she was the only family she had. Broke my heart, but once I knew she wasn't in any physical danger I could calm down a little. In the end, she pulled me into one, to tell me she was moving to Tasmania from Victoria. Now *that* was a good dream. But we're all different, like Conner, my younger brother. He knew who his mate was from the first dream. He'd met her already. He even knew where she was. But she was in a wheelchair and the woman hired to care for her was basically holding her captive. The only way Conner could see Tina was through dreams. Tina wasn't scared of men like Adele had been; he went in his human form."

"So why was last night the first time Kit pulled me into one?"

Jake took back control of the conversation. "Because to pull your mate into a dream, you need to visualize them. Kit had no idea who you were or what you looked like. All she knew was that you were from South America. She assumed you'd be from Chile as that's where she was born. The male is shown his mate, but the female has to wait for him to come to her. Kit's an independent woman, she didn't like that rule at all but it's how things are. There's nothing that can be done."

A soft beeping sound came from Jessie's pocket.

"Damn, I have to get moving. But can we meet

again?"

Jake nearly sighed in relief, his stomach was churning in a familiar way now and he knew he'd be physically sick soon.

"Sure can, Jessie. You have my phone number. Call me whenever you need to. I am the alpha of the leap here in Rosebery. I'm also the alpha of the Continental Leap of Australia. Dominic will be my successor. Both of us are here to help you learn everything about being a shifter."

"Okay. I'll give you a call then. Not sure when. Once racing starts it's intense without much free time."

"We understand. Whenever you're able, feel free to call. Good luck with the rally. Until next time."

Jake forced his legs to hold his weight as he stood to shake Jessie's hand. Jessie's emotions were calmer now. He was hopeful and happy. Although there were still some of his darker emotions in the mix, Jake wasn't too worried about him. Jessie was an intelligent man. He'd ask his questions and work it all out just fine.

Drawing in a final drag, Gabriel dropped his cigarette and ground the butt into the gravel with his boot heel. He blew out a stream of smoke as his latest partner joined him. What was his name again? Bill. Yeah, Bill Rayne.

But how long will you last, Mr Rayne?

You had to have a strong backbone, thick skin and a certain level of savageness to work for Trigger Corporation for any length of time. Anyone with a weak stomach or high sensibilities soon got weeded out.

Gabriel was one of the most senior field agents for that reason. He'd worked as a police investigator for over ten years before joining Trigger. He also had a personal motivation the others didn't. Motivation the higher ups didn't know about, not that they cared. The big-wigs of Trigger Corporation didn't give a damn why their field agents worked hard and well—they just demanded results and expected them to be delivered.

"You were right. The redhead is definitely one of them-"

"You doubted me?"

Rage clouded his mind. This stupid boy wouldn't know a shifter if it bit him on the ass, yet he'd doubted Gabriel's words.

"Ah, no. Of course not. I just wanted to make sure. Double check. You know how the higher-ups are about mistakes."

Gabriel scoffed. Yeah, the higher-ups didn't like errors being made. Especially the type where humans were caught or killed instead of shifters. Humans were of no use to them.

To avoid lashing out at the idiot, Gabriel took out another cigarette and lit up, the rasp of his lighter the only sound in the charged silence between them.

"I can tell you with one hundred percent assurance that the redhead is a shifter. I've seen her change form. Now, what we need to do tonight is work out who else around here is one. If we can find a whole group of them, the higher-ups will be pretty happy. Don't you think?"

The other man's eyes lit up. "Oh yeah. Think we might get to work in one of the facilities? No more chasing down strays around the countryside for us."

Stupid boy. He'd be lucky to live through this assignment. If a shifter didn't get him, Gabriel might just do the job himself and lay the blame on them. The kid obviously had a skewed view of what happened at Trigger's 'facilities'. Nothing good happened in those places, and Gabriel knew all too well how easily the guards could be turned into captives.

"How about you do your current job, and worry about the future later. Move around and see if you can identify any others, but don't attempt to catch any yet. Just take photos if you're able to. I'm going to keep watching our little redhead to see who she's friendly with. We'll call it in for a complete clean-up if there's more than half a dozen. It'll have to wait until after this rally is over though. We don't need to gain media attention."

"But-"

He growled and bared his teeth at the idiot. "Do. Not. Push. Me."

The younger man scurried away like the mouse he was, and Gabriel returned his attention to the redhead. She was a beautiful woman. Such a pity she was nothing more than an abomination of nature. He lifted his phone to snap a couple of pictures of her as she crossed the road and entered a hotel lobby.

Slipping his phone back in his pocket, he moved

toward the entrance. Putting out his cigarette in an ashtray outside the door, he strode through the pristine white lobby toward the function room. This *Welcoming Party* was open invitation so thankfully he didn't have to stop at the door. Keeping near the outside edge, he made his way around the room. He wanted to stay in the shadows where it wouldn't be too difficult to remain unseen and unnoticed. There was nothing tying him to any of the rally teams, so he was a nobody. Nothing but a face in the crowd, which was exactly what he wanted them to see him as. He slowly moved over to the bar.

"Pot of whatever beer's on tap. Thanks mate."

He handed over a ten-dollar note and waited for his beer and change. Once he had them, he returned to the safety of the shadows where a few other older single men were standing. He took a deep swallow of beer and settled in, leaning against a small high table. He was now comfortable that he looked like everyone else here with his partly empty glass of amber liquid and giving off a casual interest in the show. Although, calling this welcome party a show was a bit over the top. It was your typical Aussie get-together as far as he could see. A couple dozen tables, a whole heap of chairs and people milling around pretending to like others they probably spent the rest of the year bitching about.

The redhead was a social little thing, flitting around the place, chatting to everyone. He kept snapping pictures as he pretended to be focused on his phone. Later, he'd look up all the people she'd spoken with, see what he could find out about each one. There were little tells he'd learned to look for that gave it away if someone was a shifter. The main one was how they moved. Even in human form they seemed to prowl more than walk. Their sensitive nose and ears meant sharp, loud noises or strong smells would have them flinching too. It also helped that for the most part, the shifters didn't know about how much of a threat Trigger really was to them. Didn't realize they were being hunted. It was only the odd paranoid shifter that would hide all aspects of their true nature. Most shifters settled on simply not exposing their ability to the general public, because any fool could see how doing that wouldn't end well.

Kit smiled as she moved around the room feeling totally relaxed. She'd always enjoyed working the rally. Personally, she loved her Ducati motorcycle. Nothing beat roaring down the road on her bike, but she could appreciate a nice rally car. Rallying wasn't like racing. They didn't simply go around a circuit and attempt to be faster than everyone else. Rallying had corners and jumps and you raced the clock. No chance of some asshole shoving you off the road so he could beat you. You needed to keep one hundred percent control of your vehicle, or you got to meet some trees up close and personal.

The other thing that drew her in was the people. Most teams functioned like a family. Sure the odd person was full of himself, but they were easy to ignore. The rest were incredibly friendly and easy to be around.

"Kit! There you are. How are you going?"

She turned as a man she'd befriended years earlier approached to give her a quick hug.

"Barry. I'm doing well. You?"

"You know me. Same 'ol."

"I wasn't sure you'd make it this year."

He chuckled at her. "I see you're as cheeky as ever. I've got a few good years left in me, girl. I'm not that old."

"Never said you were. Just thought you'd find something better to do with your time than climb around beneath a car."

He gave her a sly grin. "I'm the mechanical engineer this year, Kit. I don't climb under the car—I'm the one who tells the young bucks what they need to do when *they* go under."

Kit chuckled as she shook her head at the older man.

"Tell me, Barry. You ever heard of Lutrec? I haven't seen him around this event before."

Barry crossed his arms over his solid chest as his eyes turned serious.

"He's got himself a solid reputation in South America, guess he's out to make a name for himself on the international circuit now. He's part of the WRC2, so only has six events this season. Pretty sure this is his last one, but don't hold me to it."

"So he's good behind the wheel. What have you heard about him outside of rallying?"

"Not much, I don't get into the who's who off the

track, you know that. Why are you asking, Kit? This bloke catch your eye?"

Kit had no idea how to explain what was going on between her and Jessie. There was basically nothing going on, yet. But they were mates. Theoretically, that meant they'd end up together so she couldn't just mouth off to Barry about him.

"Just curious, Barry. Don't go spreading any rumors just yet."

He chuckled, as she'd wanted him to. "Ah, the day you get snapped up all the single drivers will stop entering this event. I thoroughly enjoy how you shut them all down year after year."

She felt her cheeks heat a little. "No one comes all this way to look at me, and you know it. And I don't spend all my time shutting down men's advances."

He smiled at her, with that indulgent father-figure smile older men had. Jake often looked at her with the same expression. "You don't even know you're doing it, do you, Kit? You can't knock them all back forever, sweetheart. Gotta risk that tender heart of yours at some point."

Emotion pricked her eyes. Barry had always seen more than he should have.

"I know, buddy. Clock's ticking and all that."

"I might not know much about Lutrec, but I heard about Hacket mouthing off. I can tell you that boy's full of shit. Wouldn't believe him if he told me the sun was coming up tomorrow, if you get my drift."

"I sure do, thanks, Barry. I better keep moving. Only get to chat with you all once a year, gotta make sure I don't miss anyone."

Barry's gaze focused above her shoulder as his hands moved to rest on his hips. "Not sure how many others you'll get to catch up with. Looks like Lutrec has you in his sights."

Kit briefly turned her head to check out the approaching man. Damn, he scrubbed up nice. The welcoming party wasn't black tie, but it was formal enough he was sporting a shirt and tie with black dress pants.

"Thanks, Barry."

Not wanting to have an audience to any conversation she and Jessie would have, Kit moved away from the groups of people, toward the side exit. This hotel had lovely gardens and she slipped out the door into them, taking a deep breath of the crisp evening air.

"Kit! Hold up."

She stopped walking and pivoted toward him, while she focused on keeping her expression clear of all emotion. Jessie stopped a few feet away from her. His gaze ran up and down her body, making her skin tingle. Suddenly she wished she was wearing her usual t-shirt, jeans and boots. Her blue fitted button-up shirt and black dress pants, along with her three inch heels, made her feel feminine and sexy but she needed to feel tough and in control right now.

Having him this close was seriously messing with her

hormones. She was still more than a little pissed off at him for his insult in their dream, but her body was crying out for him. She eyed his lips as she ran her tongue over her own. *I wonder how he'd taste...* His groan cut short her thoughts.

"Do you have any idea what you do to me, *reinita*?"

"No, Jessie. I wouldn't have a clue. How about you tell me?"

Gah, what am I doing? Provoking him! She should be running back to the safety of her hotel room. Jessie's eyelids lowered and the left side of his mouth quirked up, bringing out the hint of a dimple in his cheek. Kit's damn heart started to pound and she could feel warmth weave through her body, settling low in her belly. He took a step toward her, and her lips parted so she could get enough air. Her lungs just wouldn't function right. What the hell was going on? This wasn't her. Kit was not a gushy girly girl. She clenched her fists and snapped her mouth shut as he stood directly in front of her. He ran a fingertip lightly down the side of her face and around her jaw.

"For the record, I do not think you are a slut, nor am I known the world over as a ladies' man. True, I'm no saint, but I hardly sleep with any woman I find who will, how did you phrase it, *open her thighs for me*."

She opened her mouth to tell him to go to hell. She felt panicky and a little out of control. She didn't like it. Before she got a sound out, his hand curled around her jaw, his thumb pressed over her lips.

"Hush, my little kitten. You don't need to spit and

claw at me. I understand you're mad, that you've been waiting for me. But I didn't know I was meant to be looking. Don't you think, that had I known you were real, not simply an incredibly beautiful figment of my imagination, that I would have come searching for you before now?"

His gaze was focused on her mouth, where he was slowly stroking his thumb back and forth. The movement froze her in place as her mind went fuzzy.

"So soft."

He slowly leaned in and replaced his thumb with his lips that were firm but gentle as he moved over her mouth. His fingers slid up her throat to cover each cheek, so her face was cradled between his palms as he tilted his head to deepen their kiss. Shivers ran over her skin and she groaned as her hands found his waist. Solid muscle twitched beneath her touch. He lightly swept the tip of his tongue along the seam of her lips, and she automatically opened for him. Her mind swirled with lust as he penetrated her mouth. Tentatively, she moved her tongue to slide against his, the feel of it causing her to moan and press her body closer to him. She needed to feel more of him, his warmth, his strength. When her breasts came into contact with his solid chest, she gasped, breaking the kiss.

Without opening his eyes or releasing his hold on Kit's face, Jessie leaned his forehead against hers. His body was on fire for her and his erection strained against his slacks, desperate to get to her. He moved his thumbs over her cheekbones as he cracked his lids open to look at her. Green eyes that were slightly slanted, making her look like the feline she was, gazed up at him looking a little shell-shocked.

"Jessie, we have to stop."

With a sigh he pulled back, gently caressing her face as he stepped away. He knew she was right. This garden was somewhat secluded, but hardly private.

"Sorry, *reinita*. That got a little heated. I can't seem to help myself."

He wondered if it was because they were mates that he couldn't keep away from her. The skin over his hips burned from where she'd held on to him while they kissed. Jessie paced around a little, never straying far from where Kit stood. Her taste had scorched its way down his throat. He was certain no other female would do it for him now. She smelled of a mix of spice and vanilla, and his senses were filled with it now.

Jessie had been happy with his life before he had met Kit. He liked having the freedom of being single. No ties to anywhere in particular, he could roam as he chose. He'd thought it was because of his leopard that he craved solitude. Had he been unintentionally searching? Since meeting her, his heart didn't ache for him to move on like it normally did. He'd been in Tasmania for just on a week now, and normally by this point he had to focus on the race, his work, all the people on his team he'd let down if he just up and left.

He didn't feel any of that now. Something deep within him had altered. He felt almost content. At the realization, his palms grew damp with sweat while his stomach clenched into knots of fear. He frowned as he glanced over at Kit. She stood still, two fingers gently rubbing her lips, which were red from his kiss. Her behavior was that of someone who'd never been kissed before. Her other arm was wrapped around her slender waist protectively and her gaze was wary as she watched him pace around her.

"I need to go. I can't. I just can't do this. Sorry."

Knowing his apology was lame, but unable to say anything more, he bolted for the door and rushed through the now crowded room. He ignored Pedro calling his name as he made his way to the other side of the hotel where the rooms were located. He was in a full-out panic by the time he reached his room. He had to hold his breath to get his hand steady enough to slide the key card home. Once inside the safety of his room, he took a couple of deep breaths.

Kit had told him as much in their dream, but her reaction to his kiss confirmed it without a doubt. She was a virgin. So fucking innocent. She wasn't a bit of fun like his other lovers had been. Even if he ignored all the mate crap, he knew she was special. Kit was the kind of woman you took and kept forever. She'd be protective and loving and stand beside him. But he didn't want a wife, or rather, he didn't want to be a husband. He was petrified he'd become his father. He stumbled across the floor, landing awkwardly on the bed as memories sucked him under.

He was back in his childhood bedroom on the morning of his fifteenth birthday. He sat naked on the floor in the center of his room trembling in shock and fear; it had only been a couple of hours since he'd first changed into a large cat. His bedroom door swung open and his mother strode in, carrying a small wrapped parcel. Her smile fell, and she dropped to her knees beside him.

She put a palm to his forehead before she spoke in their native Spanish, "My son, are you not well?"

He struggled to find the words to explain. "Mama, I'm scared."

"Tell me what happened, what has you so frightened? And where are your clothes?"

She gasped as she picked up shreds of cloth from the floor beside him.

"I don't know. I'll try to show you."

Earlier he'd managed to turn back by wishing he were human, so he got on all fours and closed his eyes while focusing on being a cat. He felt the tingle in his limbs and opened his eyes to see blue light surrounding him. His mother's breath hitched and she called out for Felipe, his father, in a panicked voice.

"What's all the bloody yelling about in here? You both know I don't have time for this shit in the morning-"

His voice cut short as he stomped into the room. Focusing once again, Jessie changed back to human and shivered under the intense stare of his father. Jessie held his breath, unsure how his father would react. He was a violent man who easily flew into a rage. He would lash out at both Jessie and his mother without warning on a regular basis.

Jessie cringed as Felipe sneered and he turned his attention to his wife, Jessie's mother.

"How dare you lay with another man then have me raise the bastard!"

A loud crack filled the air as Felipe slapped his mother, bloodying her lip and knocking her from where she knelt to the floor.

"Felipe, you can see for yourself he is your son. Look at him, he has your eyes, your hair. I have never once cheated on you, as well you know."

His mother's voice was quiet and gentle. Jessie knew she was trying to soothe him. He also knew it wasn't going to work and tears stung his eyes at what was to come. Jessie fought to keep the moisture locked inside, knowing better than to let them fall. His father despised weakness of any sort in his son.

This was not the first time Jessie had seen his father make his mother bleed. If he looked close enough at his mother on any given day, he could see the bruises and welts from his father's temper. The only thing that would make this encounter different would be if he stopped after just one hit. Jessie prayed his father would stop. That he would get angry enough that he would storm out of the house and work off his frustration somewhere else.

Felipe had never been good at controlling any of his impulses. Jessie had heard the talk around town of all the women his father had been with. Fury built inside of Jessie as he thought of how Felipe slept with whomever he wanted but his mother was expected to be faithful.

"It must be magic then, Tatiana. You've been messing with black magic? There's no other explanation. What was your aim? Did you hope to have him turn into a beast and kill me? Is being my wife such a trial? I put food in your bellies and a roof over your heads, what more do you require?"

Felipe took a fist full of his mother's hair and pulled her roughly to her feet. Tears streamed down her face as she raised her hands to attempt to pry his fingers from her hair. The move revealed her forearms along with the wide red welts that Jessie knew came from his father's belt. He'd sported the same marks often enough. Felipe used his grip in her hair to give her a shake and Jessie's anger mounted to unprecedented levels. Whatever had happened to him overnight had fortified him, made him stronger and braver. And he was sick and tired of seeing his precious mama be brutalized by this bastard.

"No answer?"

With that one sentence, Jessie's composure snapped and he rose to stand up to his father.

"Leave her alone. She's done nothing. She never does anything but see the back of your hand! It's you that sleeps around, Papa! It's you that vents your fury at her, not the other way around."

The second the words left his mouth he knew he'd made a mistake. His mind might be stronger, but his body wasn't. Felipe was a big man and had no problem using his size to his advantage. Jessie winced as his father roughly shoved his mother hard against the wall where she hit with a loud thump before she slid to the ground weeping quietly as she cradled her shoulder. Jessie hoped she hadn't dislocated it again, but before he could go to her, Felipe turned on him.

"Is that right, son? You think you're man enough to take me on now, do you? I'll soon teach you a lesson, boy. Perhaps it was you that has messed with black magic. Huh? Is that what happened?"

Jessie didn't respond. He knew no words would appease his father. Without warning Felipe punched him in the stomach and when Jessie hunched forward, he landed a hard blow between his shoulder blades. Agony engulfed him as he screamed out and crumpled to the floor.

"Pathetic. You think a man cries when he's hit? Learn to take the pain, boy. Then you'll be a man. Hell, your mother takes it better than you. Let me show you."

As Felipe used his mother's good arm to wrench her from the floor, she cried out a pained sound, which pushed Jessie past his limit. He allowed his fury to descend over him. A flash of blue filled his vision and he knew he was a feline once again. This time he didn't fear his new form, he relished the power it gave him. He growled low, and his father spun back toward him, releasing his mother so she slumped to the floor away from Felipe. Jessie bared his teeth at the clear shot he now had at his father.

"What the fuck do you think you're doing, boy?"

I'm finishing this. *He leapt and landed his front paws against his father's solid chest, taking him down hard to the floor. Felipe's strong hands pulled and pushed at Jessie's thick neck, but he could barely feel it through his thick fur. Without further thought Jessie wrapped his mouth around the soft throat in front of him and ripped it free. As blood sprayed over his face, reality came crashing down.*

He'd killed his father!

He stumbled away and tripped over his feet. He allowed his body to fall limply to the floor as he sobbed. He was vaguely aware of his mother coming over to him. He felt her trembling fingers in his fur and felt her tears land on him.

"Shhh, it'll be okay, Jessie. He can't hurt either of us anymore. Shhh, my son."

Jessie came back to reality in a rush. He flew up from the bed and ran into the bathroom, barely making it to the toilet in time to empty his stomach. He would never regret protecting his mother, but the guilt of taking his father's life still rode him hard if he allowed the memories to surface. He knew now, as he'd known then, that it had to be done. It was truly a case of either his father or his mother who was going to walk out of his bedroom that day. He simply wished his father had been a better man, that he'd not been so cruel as to force his son's hand.

An image of Kit filled his mind. She was pure, innocent and beyond beautiful. He couldn't bear it if he caused her harm. What if he was like his father? What if after the honeymoon phase was over, he got possessive and began hurting her? His mother had told him his father had once been tender and sweet with her.

Chapter Three

With her stomach in knots, Kit stomped around the checkpoint. She must look as awful as she felt as no one had spoken to her all morning, which was highly unusual. She'd had no appetite for the past couple days and hadn't bothered to force food into her stomach. That probably hadn't been the best idea, but she couldn't face eating. Jessie had her so bloody confused. It had become beyond obvious that Jessie was avoiding her. She'd barely seen him since things got a little hot five days ago at the welcome dinner. Damn, for a first kiss, it was certainly memorable. She rolled her lips in over her teeth as she remembered how he'd taken her mouth. Arousal wound its way through the other emotions swirling in her mind and she growled. Dammit! She needed to keep a clear head, and not let all this hormonal emotional crap get to her. She was a grown woman and she could control her own mind, in theory. In reality it seemed she actually didn't have much control over anything.

Even though Jessie hadn't spoken to her and she'd not even seen him since that night, she had felt him watching her. Whenever they were on break or she was manning a checkpoint he was coming through, she knew his gaze was focused on her. There was only one more full day of racing after today… What would he do when it was over? Would he just leave, pretend like he'd never met her? Or was he going to give them a chance? At this point she didn't know what she wanted him to do. For the first time in a very long time she was afraid and completely uncertain about what she should do.

With a sigh, she rubbed the bridge of her nose. At least this stage of the rally was near Rosebery. Conner had texted her earlier saying he was bringing Tina up to have lunch with them. She'd make sure she ate with them. That should help her cope with all this shit. She knew better than to try to function at full capacity on an empty stomach. Although, seeing Tina would bring back the other reason her mood was in the crapper. Robyn was still on the loose. The crazy bitch had been pulling increasingly insane stunts to gain Tina's father's attention. Kit was worried it would cost someone their life soon.

Racing was currently halted so everyone could have some lunch. Kit decided to give the guys a break from her bad attitude and headed toward the toilet block. She needed a few minutes away from being under Jessie's intense stare. Why wouldn't the damn man just talk to her? She stopped short as she rounded a large tree. Robyn stood behind Tina, a hand in the wheelchair-bound woman's hair. Kit couldn't see the other hand as she silently crept toward them, but she could smell blood in the air.

"Maybe I don't need to do anymore. I do believe I've done enough. There is a lot of blood and you are looking a little pale."

Fury flowed through Kit, clearing her mind, focusing her sight and giving her extra strength. Kit had confronted Robyn at the hospital a few weeks ago and warned her to stay away. She mentally kicked herself for not following her instincts and taking care of the bitch then and there. If Tina died, she'd never forgive herself for showing mercy to Robyn that day.

The bitch was so focused on her prey she didn't notice Kit approaching. Using her supernatural speed, she gripped Robyn's wrist that was connected to the hand buried in Tina's blonde hair. The woman growled as Kit pressed hard on a pressure point that had Robyn releasing Tina, and quite probably breaking her wrist.

"What the hell?"

Ignoring Robyn's comment, Kit gripped her arm and spun her away from Tina. Stupid woman stumbled and fell to her knees with a cry of pain. A moment later, Robyn's hate-filled gaze lifted to focus on Kit.

"You piece of shit. I told you if you hurt her, I'd make you pay."

Kit stepped forward as she spoke, dropping into a low fighter's stance while pulling back her arm ready to strike. With the way Robyn was kneeling, her jaw was the perfect height and angle for what she planned to do. With every ounce of her strength, she swung her arm up and delivered a perfectly executed uppercut to the bitch's jaw. Being a shifter had its benefits, added strength being one of them. She watched in satisfaction as Robyn crumpled to the ground and stayed there, out cold.

She turned to see Conner and Dale both with Tina. Her shirt was soaked with blood and Conner had his hands around her neck. It was obvious Robyn had attempted to slice open her throat. With a growl, Kit turned back toward the bitch; she was going to finish her for good. Make sure there was no way she could hurt Tina again.

She stilled as she took in what was happening before her. Jessie was kneeling on the ground next to Robyn, wrapping a rope around her wrists, which he had pulled behind her back. He was dead calm as he finished tying her up. Kit couldn't process how she felt. He undoubtedly just saved Robyn's life, maybe saved Kit from doing time for murder too.

She rested her hands on her hips and bumped into her radio, which rapidly shifted her focus. Tina was hurt and needed medical attention. Grabbing the radio, she put in a call back to base, quickly requested both ambulance and police attendance at their location. In hindsight, killing Robyn really wasn't the right thing to do. Now that some of the rage had drained from her system, she knew she'd have regretted her decision if she'd been allowed to follow through on it.

"Owe you a drink or twenty, Kit."

Conner's hoarse voice pulled her focus away from her

inner turmoil and she walked over to him.

"Nah, I got to rough her up some. That's reward in itself. Not that I'd turn down a free drink or two."

Conner looked broken, not at all the strong and confident man he normally was. She gave her leap brother's shoulder a squeeze, willing some of her strength into him. A low growl filled the air and Conner jerked his gaze over toward Jessie.

"Ah, Kit? What's the go with that?"

Yeah, she wouldn't mind knowing what was going on with Jessie either. She released Conner's shoulder and turned to look at her mate.

"Ah, yeah. That would be rally driver, Jessie Lutrec. Apparently he's my mate. Not sure he likes the idea, though."

"Why wouldn't he?"

Kit clenched her jaw as she recalled all the times Jake had told her no one would treat her differently if they knew her secret. It was becoming clear that it was only a matter of time until it was revealed. Jessie's complete lack of knowledge about shifters was going to give him away, and by extension, Kit. She faced Conner, holding his gaze as she threw it out there.

"Because he doesn't understand. He's a new shifter, conceived with the last comet passing. I get the feeling he's never found another shifter until me."

She watched emotions flicker across Conner's face. Shock, confusion, but no rejection or judgment. A spark of relief flared within her but before Conner could verbally respond, the sounds of sirens stirred the air and he turned his full attention back to his injured mate. Her adrenaline was wearing off and she felt light headed all of a sudden so she stood back as everyone helped get Tina off to hospital and Robyn into the police paddy wagon. Robyn was conscious now, but very subdued. Bitch probably had a concussion. The police mentioned they were going to take her over to the hospital at Strahan as Tina was on her way to the one in Rosebery. Probably a good idea or they'd be arresting Conner for murder.

"Kit?"

She closed her eyes and let her head fall forward. She did not have the energy to fight Jessie at the moment. His large warm palm slid around her ribs and came to rest over her tummy. She'd taken off her heavy uniform jacket so she felt every ounce of Jessie's heat through the thin black t-shirt she wore. She let him pull her back until she was flush against his solid chest for a moment. She'd waited four years for him to show up and now that he had, part of her wanted to just fall into his embrace and stay there. But life in the real world wasn't that simple and self-preservation had her reluctantly pulling away from him. She took a deep breath before she headed back toward the rally without uttering a word. She had a job to do, and that's what she needed to focus on. Not her mixed emotions that felt like they just got put through a blender.

"There's so many of them! We'll never be able to round them all up for transport."

Bill tossed the photo he'd been looking at on to the table with all the others. It seemed everywhere they turned they found more shifters. He looked over at his partner, who sat motionless, staring at a photo of the redheaded firefighter. Bill was getting so tired of Gabriel's obsession with that chick. She definitely needed to be dealt with first. Once she was out of the way, they could focus on the rest of them.

"So, where do you think we should start?"

"With so many, I need to call it in. Find out what the higher-ups want to do."

Bill shuddered, suddenly very glad Gabriel outranked him. The older man drove him nuts for the most part with all his serious silence. But if it meant Bill didn't have to speak with the higher -ups personally, then it was worth putting up with. For now, anyway.

Gabriel cleared his throat and rolled his shoulders as he held his phone to his ear. Hell, the higher-ups were scary enough to have even big, tough Gabriel sweating. Bill was grateful he'd been recruited by another field operative, not the higher-ups, when he started with Trigger, so he'd not yet caught their attention. So far, his jobs consisted of going on hunts where he shot tranquilizer guns and helped cage big cats. He wasn't the smartest man around, he knew it as well as everyone else, so he was happy being a grunt. Mind you, if they pulled this one off, maybe he could be a grunt in one of the underground facilities. All this running around and fresh air got boring after a while. A nice cushy lab job sounded all right to him.

"Gabriel here, sir. We have a situation that I need you to advise me how to handle."

As Gabriel relayed the situation, Bill began sorting the photos. There were four men, two had to be at least brothers if not twins, plus the redhead. They were all firefighters volunteering at the rally. That rally driver, Lutrec, who kept hanging around the redhead was suspicious. He didn't behave like a typical shifter, but there was definitely something strange about the man. That put his co-driver in question too, although from what he'd seen, that guy seemed all human. He moved with no fluidity or grace and his reflexes weren't as fast as Lutrec's. They needed to study him some more to be sure.

When they'd heard about a disturbance at one of the rally check points over their police scanner, they'd gone to the place to discover an ambulance officer and at least three other males who were also shifters. There were also a few more suspects that like the co-driver, required further investigating.

Gabriel hung up the phone with a sigh.

"They'll get back to us with a plan. Until then, we need to start identifying some of them. If we can nail down locations, we may be able to start picking off the odd one without gaining too much attention."

"Well, I've sorted these photos into the two groups, definites and potentials. Want me to start looking into these potentials? See if I can identify for certain if they are shifter or human?"

"No, I'll do that. I have more years of experience picking them out than you. You see if you can work out when these confirmed shifters are alone. Try to work out their schedules, any repetitive behavior. We'll also need to do a stock-take of what we have in weapons and storage."

Great. An afternoon of counting shit in a shed, checking weapons followed by an evening of trolling the internet. Woo hoo, another night for the record books. He held in his sigh as he cracked his knuckles.

"Guess I'll go start counting cages then."

Bill's temper was rising and he needed to be away from Gabriel before he lost it and flattened the smug bastard. Maybe he'd just take out that redhead later, get even with him that way. Obviously he had a crush on the chick or something.

On autopilot, Jessie geared up. The familiar process of putting on all the fireproof gear, then his overalls, helped him clear his mind a little. He couldn't shake what he'd seen yesterday. He'd finished the morning stages and was watching everyone avoid Kit as she paced around in a foul mood. He was waiting for an opportunity to get her alone. When she'd walked off toward the toilet block, he'd thought it would be the perfect chance to chat with her and had jogged over to catch up to her. They needed to talk; he'd only left her alone during the week as he'd needed his full attention on the rally, but now with one day left he found he couldn't keep away from her any longer.

Jessie had smelled the blood at the same moment Kit went perfectly still. He'd looked past Kit to see a woman in a wheelchair being held by another woman standing behind her. The sunlight glinted off a knife that lay in front of them in the dirt. Glancing back at Kit, he'd seen she was prowling toward them. A magnificent sight, no doubt about it, all that coiled rage and power. He'd briefly left her to it while he went looking for something to tie up the other woman. He'd heard a little about Kit's reputation and was confident she wouldn't get herself hurt while he was gone.

He'd returned in time to see Kit deliver one single uppercut that knocked the woman out. He'd frozen in shock for a moment. He'd never known a woman who could do so much damage. Kit turned toward the injured lady in the chair, then growled as she returned her focus on the unconscious woman. He'd quickly dropped down and pulled her hands behind her back to tie them. The look on Kit's face hadn't been good. She'd been out for blood and apparently she had the ability and skills to acquire it.

Fortunately, tying the woman up had the desired effect of calming Kit out of her murderous rage. He wouldn't wish the guilt associated with taking a life on anyone, especially this woman. One he couldn't seem to get out of his head.

"Hey, Jessie. You okay, *amigo*?"

Jessie shook his head to clear it and sat down to put his boots on.

"I'm fine. Just thinking."

"About yesterday? You want to talk it out?"

"What's to say? You saw what happened yourself."

"Yeah, Kit saved that young woman's life. Protected her. From what you told me about how your kind was created, isn't that the point? Aren't you all meant to be protectors?"

Clenching his jaw, Jessie looked up into Pedro's gaze. "What if I'm like my father?"

Pedro's eyes went wide as he gasped, "That's what has you tangled up? You're scared you're like your old man?"

With a low growl, Jessie scrubbed his face in his palms.

"You know full well it's what I've always been afraid of. I don't want to be like him, hurting those I should care for."

"Jessie, you are nothing like your father. You scored some of his looks from what I've heard, but it's your mother's tender heart that rules your life. You know, it's eighty percent environment and only twenty percent genetics that determines how a child will turn out. Your mother raised you, even before your father died, it was her. You would never raise a hand to someone you cared for."

Jessie glanced up as Pedro started chuckling. "What's funny?"

"Just thinking of what that woman would do if you did

try to pull some shit. *Amigo*, she'd have you on your ass before you knew what happened."

Jessie's lip quirked a little. Yeah, Kit would have no qualms about putting him in his place if he stepped out of line. Maybe they had a chance after all. Even if it turned out that he did have a little of his old man in him.

"Yeah, she would. Come on, let's get this show on the road. Final day already."

Pedro let the subject drop and clapped Jessie on the shoulder before he left the tent. Jessie needed to focus on the race, not Kit, until the rally was over. He'd finish today's stages, then he'd worry about his girl. He grabbed his helmet and gloves before he followed after Pedro. He approached his red and white Subaru and felt the buzz flow through his blood. He loved what he did. Rally driving was what he lived for. Tight corners, open roads...the need to have one hundred percent control over his vehicle. He closed his eyes and took a deep breath as he adjusted his balaclava, then slid his helmet on. His team manager, Luan, approached and helped secure the straps on his helmet and checked his HANS was connected to his helmet correctly and resting over his collarbones as it should. The thing was a little uncomfortable but he'd seen the difference it could make in a crash so was happy to wear it.

"Right. You're all set, Jessie. Remember what you learned from our recce, listen to Pedro and stay focused. You do well today and you might land yourself a top three placing for this event."

Damn, he'd not checked where he was ranked after yesterday's racing. He'd timed well in each stage. Well, he'd timed better in the morning than the afternoon but that was to be expected after seeing Kit do her thing.

He needed to push aside everything. Focus on the race. He began running over what he and Pedro had learned about this stage in recce. It had a sharp right after a blind crest and several other aspects he needed to keep in mind. He climbed in his car and buckled himself in before putting on his gloves.

"Pedro, you good to go?"

"Sure am. Spoke with the safety crew and have updated the pace-notes. Nothing major has changed since our recce."

He waited for his lead mechanic to give him the go ahead and then he slowly drove out of the service area toward their starting point. Once they'd taken off, with Pedro's strong, deep voice in his ear reading out their pace-notes, Jessie managed to stay focused on the road. He grinned as the car flew over a rise and caught a second or two of air. Half a dozen camera flashes twinkled from the media zone as he landed and took off around the next corner. He wondered if he'd make the highlight reel at the dinner with that jump. What would Kit think-

"Jessie! Wake the fuck up!"

Pedro's sharp alarmed voice, speaking Spanish not English, cleared his mind in an instant causing him to jerk the wheel. The rear tire hit the gravel and pulled at the vehicle. Jessie tightened his grip on the wheel as he struggled for control as the rear fishtailed out to the side. Not wanting to roll, he allowed the car to spin around. Finally it came to a stop when their rear left bumper hit the embankment. Fortunately, they'd not had much speed and when he gunned the engine it took off up the road with no issues. But they had some serious time to make up for now.

"Sorry, Pedro. I'll try to get the seconds back."

With his heart pounding in his chest and adrenaline from the near crash flowing through his veins, he was one hundred percent about the race as they finished the stage in what he hoped was record time.

Kit stood on guard at the Stop Control. Jessie should be on the track now. With the two-minute break between starts, she figured she'd see one or two cars cross the line before him, assuming they didn't crash out. This stage had lots of twists and turns, along with trees close to the road. It was notorious for claiming vehicles. Maybe that's why she felt on edge. Something was off but she couldn't put her finger on it. She frowned. Maybe she was just worried about Tina, although, she was fine now. Well, she would be soon. Now she was fully mated to Conner, she'd heal faster than a normal human and recover from her neck wound in no time. And Robyn was locked up so she no longer posed a threat to Tina.

The sound of an engine coming closer had her looking up to the flying finish line in time to watch a dark green

VW Golf cross the line. It pulled up perfectly and the scrutineers rushed over to them to do what they did for each car.

Kit crossed her arms as she shifted her weight from one foot to the other. There wasn't much for her to do as fire marshal at this stage. By day five, whatever was going to go wrong with the cars had, for the most part, already happened. Notwithstanding crashes, of course.

Rustling in the scrub behind her caught Kit's attention a second before a solid arm wrapped around her throat. Shock allowed her attacker a moment to tighten his hold on her and Kit felt his moist breath on her ear as he spoke quietly.

"Don't make a sound, or I'll snap your pretty little neck."

Her instincts flared to life and all her training kicked in. His hand was clamped on to her shoulder with his forearm pressed across her windpipe. She moved her head to the side so the front of her throat was in his elbow, which allowed her to calmly take a deep breath. She shifted her feet into a wider stance as she quickly raised her hand and grabbed his pinky finger. Kit pulled it back hard as she spun out of his hold. The man cursed as he cradled his injured hand. Kit didn't think. She struck out hard and fast with a quick jab at his nose. He flinched away and she caught his cheek. He stumbled back toward the tree line with a curse as she heard an engine roar behind her.

Still on high alert she spun in time to see Jessie's car

skid to a stop and him ripping at his harness trying to get free of the vehicle. She turned back to refocus on her attacker to see him fleeing through the bush. Her first instinct was to chase the bastard down, but then she caught sight of the logo over his bicep. *Fuck.* She'd seen that stylized eye before. Back when she was fifteen, hours before Jake and Sophie had found her, she'd seen three men setting large traps in the bush where she'd been hiding. She'd heard them mention how easy it would be to catch the young leopard they'd been told about. When she'd seen them pull out guns, she'd snuck away.

Once out of their hearing range, she'd run. As fast as she could, she'd kept on running until her legs refused to continue. Only then did she stop and that was where Choden, Jake and Sophie had found her. Before she'd exerted herself, Kit had been hungry and thirsty. Afterward she'd felt weak and disorientated. She'd been stumbling around trying to make her way through the bush when she'd seen the three of them. She'd frozen with panic until Sophie had shifted to a large snow leopard. Desperate for nourishment and friendly company, she'd allowed them to take her with them. Best decision she'd ever made.

"Kit? What the hell was that?"

Jessie's deep voice pulled her free from her memories and she began to stalk over to the scrutineers' tent where all the officials were watching her closely with concern.

"It was nothing, Jessie. Some punk thought I was an easy mark. He found out I'm not."

Jessie growled low but wisely didn't continue his questions. From the corner of her eye, she saw him storm over to his car before driving it over to the where he should be. She rolled her eyes when he once again left Pedro with the vehicle to come back to her.

Kit knew on the outside she looked as cool and calm as she always did when everyone went back to whatever they were meant to be doing. She was grateful they all believed that nothing was going on other than some young kid had tried a move and got the beating he deserved. On the inside was a different story. That logo was Trigger Corporation's calling card, but why were they here? From what she'd managed to find out, Trigger were organized in their attacks on shifters. They didn't do spur of the moment, which is what today had been. That thug had seen an opportunity and had taken it. Maybe he was a new recruit? Out without his partner.

"Who was that?"

Once again Jessie pulled her from her thoughts. He was standing close in front of her and looked completely riled up. Apparently he didn't believe her when she'd said it was nothing.

"Not a clue. And here is not the time or the place to discuss it, understand?"

She could see he was grinding his teeth by the movement in his strong jaw. Damn but the man was well put together, and very, very distracting. Part of her, a tiny hidden inner part, craved him and wanted nothing more than to fall into his arms and let him shelter her. But her tough inner core that had always protected her wouldn't allow it. Fate might have dictated they were mates, but she wasn't going to instantly put all her trust and faith in the guy. Especially since he couldn't seem to decide if he wanted her or not. His hot and cold treatment toward her was giving her a headache.

"Honestly, I'm surprised you care, Jessie. I mean, you kiss me then run off like your tail is on fire. Ignore me for days, and now you're attempting to go caveman on my ass. Like I'm yours to protect or some shit."

Pain flashed across his features before he quickly buried it.

"Kit, it's been a damn big week. I've discovered that I'm not the only— Shit, Kit, this isn't a conversation we need to have in public."

"Guess you'll have to see me outside of the rally then, won't you?"

He frowned a little. "I have no problem with that, Kit. You want to meet up for dinner tonight? We can get a table at the back of the hotel restaurant. No one will over hear us if we keep our voices low."

She rubbed the bridge of her nose. "Yeah. Okay. Dinner tonight."

Kit had some questions of her own. Like what the hell were his plans after racing finished tomorrow?

Chapter Four

All afternoon nervous energy had Jessie restless and unable to settle down. The fact someone had tried to hurt Kit didn't sit well with him. He'd not had a good look at the guy as the bastard had been running away— undoing the six-point harness and getting out of a rally car wasn't a simple task. All the safety measures had never bothered him before. But in that moment, when he'd flown past the finish line and seen Kit being held hostage by a man, he'd seen red and couldn't get to her fast enough.

Instead of stopping at the scrutineers' station, he'd raced over to her. But in the minutes it took him to get to her, she'd dealt with the situation. Again. Seemed to Jessie that Kit was completely self-sufficient. What the hell was he meant to do with her? He looked down at his watch. He still had a few hours before he was meeting Kit. Maybe another chat with Jake before he spoke with Kit again was a good idea.

When he got back to his room at the hotel, he fell into a chair and dialed the number Jake had given him.

"Jake White."

"*Hola,* Jake, Jessie here. You got a minute or two?"

"Sure, son, what's on your mind?"

Jessie roughly scrubbed his free hand over his face as he sighed into the phone. How to put it into words?

"How about I take a guess? You got issues with Kit, son?"

A slight grin tugged at his mouth. "How'd you guess?"

"I know that girl all too well, and I always knew she'd be a handful for her mate."

"Honestly, I don't know that the woman needs a man at all!"

"She needs you more than either of you probably realize. There's a lot more to Kit than her tough exterior, Jessie."

"Yeah, well, that tough exterior is made out of kryptonite or something."

The older man sighed. "She's had to learn to keep her walls high and strong. As you know, being a comet shifter has extra difficulties the rest of us never have to deal with."

Jessie didn't need the reminder. "Yeah, my fifteenth birthday was all rainbows and sunshine."

"I can imagine, and if you ever need to talk about what happened, you know where to find me. Or if you want someone younger to chat with, Dominic is always around."

"Maybe one day, but honestly, I do my best to not think about it at all."

"Kit has never told me exactly what happened to her after her first shift. But when I found her, she wasn't in a good place."

Jessie rubbed his eyes and pushed the memories down. He didn't need to relive them again so soon after having dreamt it. He wondered what had happened to Kit with hers. They really hadn't spoken about themselves much at all since they'd met.

"Don't suppose you feel like telling me?"

Jake clucked his tongue. "I wish I could, son. I truly do. But that's something she needs to tell you herself. What I can assure you is that it was no picnic for her either. If you want to know what happened, I'd suggest you start by offering up your own experience. Could be the common ground you're looking for to start her opening up to you."

Damn, surely there was something lighter to discuss with her than that! He didn't think leading with a tale on how he murdered his father was going to help forge a relationship of any kind with Kit.

"Yeah, I'll think about it. Listen, while we're talking, don't suppose you know of anyone who would be gunning for Kit?"

The older man's voice grew serious, "What do you mean, Jessie?"

"This afternoon at the end of a stage, I crossed the finish line to see some man trying to pull Kit into the trees. Naturally she kicked his butt and got herself free before I could get over to her."

He clenched his jaw with the frustration of yet again not being able to protect Kit, before he forced his muscles to relax and he blew out a breath. Why the hell did he even care that he couldn't protect her? She hadn't been injured in the encounter. That was what was important.

"You see anything distinctive about him?"

"The bastard ran off into the bush before I got a good look at him, but I can tell you that he wore a black short sleeve shirt with an eye looking logo over both upper arms. That mean anything to you?"

Jessie winced at Jake's curse. Jake was silent a few moments before he spoke in a tight voice.

"Yeah, son. I know exactly what that logo means. You ever heard of Trigger Corporation?"

"Can't say I have, who are they?"

"Nothing good. You need to stay clear of them. You see that logo or the name Trigger, you get the bloody hell away from them as fast as you can. Understand me? Do not draw attention to yourself around them, and get away."

Jessie frowned at the sternness in Jake's voice. "Okay. But why?"

"Listen, Jessie. If Trigger are in the area I need to let the whole leap know, and fast. Especially if they're already attacking us. After I get a plan in place, if you want, I'll sit down with you and explain everything I know about them, which sadly isn't much. Looking into them too deeply would attract their attention. Which every shifter wants to avoid. So I haven't delved into researching them."

Jake's voice had gone even rougher with emotion.

Jessie hadn't ever heard the man to be anything but completely level and calm. If Trigger were scary enough to have Jake on edge, Jessie would heed the man's advice and stay clear of them.

"Jake, would Kit know about Trigger?"

"Honestly, I'm not sure. She's never asked me about them, but she's always kept a lot of things to herself. Did Kit say she knew who he was?"

"No, she told me she didn't have a clue who he was, then went on to say it wasn't the place to discuss it. We're meeting for dinner in about an hour."

A heavy sigh came over the line. "Well, I'm going to make these calls. Let me know if Kit knows anything about the man after her, okay?"

"Sure, Jake. Can't see Kit telling me much, but I intend to try to get her to tell me if she knows who it might have been."

He hung up and headed straight for his laptop. He needed to see what he could find out about this Trigger crowd before he saw Kit. If they were already here, doing a general search wasn't going to raise any flags that weren't already up.

Hanging up his phone, Jake rose from his seat in a jerky move. Unable to contain his frustration or anger, he roared as he shifted before he began stalking around the room. Glancing out the window, he wished he could go outside for a run, but the days were long this time of year and it was still light. The risk of being seen was too high to chance. Jake heard a gasp and turned to see that Sophie had rushed into the room.

"Jake? What's happened?"

She came to him, his precious mate, and dropped to her knees before him, sinking her hands into the thick fur of his neck.

Trigger.

With that one word, Sophie's composure shattered. Color drained from her face as she stilled. The wave of fear and sadness that came from her caused Jake's stomach to tighten. Damn, he hated how his enhanced empathy made him ill.

"No. No. Not them."

Taking a step away from her, he shifted so he could hold her. Tears ran down her cheeks and she trembled as he held her close, her wet cheek resting against his heart. He had no doubt she was remembering what he was from when they first met.

Sophie wasn't a native Tasmanian. She'd been born and raised in Broome, in the upper northwest corner of the Australian mainland. Jake had gone looking for his mate when the dreams got too much. Like Dominic with Adele, he'd felt her pain, and with his heightened empathy, it'd made him terribly sick. Thankfully, she was a shifter and knew who he was when he'd dream bonded with her. She'd told him exactly where to find her. Along with a desperate plea to hurry, and to bring backup.

Back then his father had been the alpha of the leap and

he'd sent Jake and a small group of their strongest shifters up to help battle whatever it was that was happening in Broome.

The flight they'd taken was the fastest way to get to Broome but Jake was still uneasy that he'd taken too long. The moment they were free of the airport and inside their hired car, Jake broke every speed limit to get to his mate. Deep in his soul he knew she was in serious trouble.

"Stop the car here."

Ron gripped his shoulder from where he sat in the back seat.

"It's too quiet, isn't it?"

He pulled over and hid the vehicle behind a patch of dense shrub. The other four shifters followed his lead as he opened the door and slid out. Staying close to the bush next to the road, they walked into the town where Sophie told him her leap lived.

There was no activity. No cars on the road, no people hanging around. As they passed through the outskirts into the main part of town, they found utter devastation and Jake threw up at the overload of emotion. Please don't let me have been too late.

When they found the first of the mauled human bodies along with dead snow leopards, Jake and the others all shifted to their stronger animal forms.

"This doesn't look good, boys."

"Damn straight, the place is a ghost town."

Jake guessed any humans in town would have fled at

the first signs of fighting, leaving only shifters and whoever this enemy was. Jake struggled to keep himself level. The fear and anger in the air bombarded his body, mind and soul. Fortunately, his need to find and save his mate allowed him to push it down and focus on the task at hand.

With his mind now solely focused on finding Sophie, he led his small team to the home she'd told him belonged to her family.

We need to keep silent. No growling or roaring. Follow me. Sophie gave me directions to her house.

With his warning issued, they'd moved forward as quietly as possible and kept a look out for anyone. They all knew they'd save all they could, but Jake's mate came first. As they'd drawn near, he'd pulled up short and along with the others stepped up close behind some trees. There were five men, all dressed in black leather vests with 'Trigger' embroidered across the upper back, positioned around the front of the house, guns aimed at the windows and door.

Who the hell was Trigger?

Never heard of them, let's worry about that later.

Jake had thought the same question John had voiced, but now wasn't the time to discuss it. Taking in the men, Jake guessed the back door would be similarly guarded. He didn't know how long this standoff had been going on but at some point these bastards would get sick of waiting and start shooting.

We need to do this fast and silent. We take one each at

the same time then we need to go around the back and clear out any there. This standoff isn't going to hold.

His males were good. In full stealth mode, they would be able take out the five guards at the same time. Jake counted down the attack.

Three, two, one, go!

Jake pounced and wrapping his powerful jaws around the man's throat, he crushed his windpipe. Quick and silent, the bastard was dead. He glanced around to see the other's had done the same as himself and all the men had been taken out before any alarm could be raised by them. The shock of being attacked from behind fortunately meant they all dropped their rifles without pulling triggers.

They all returned to the shadows and moved around to the back to deal with the bastards out there in a similar fashion.

Once he was certain all the enemy were down, Jake approached the house. As he padded up the front steps, he was careful to avoid the shards of glass from the broken windows.

Sophie? It's Jake. It's all clear now. Can you let us in?

He heard the shifting of something heavy then the door swung in, revealing his beautiful alpha mate standing with a rifle in her hand. As he moved in toward her, he saw the cupboard that had been blocking the door. A glance up the central hallway revealed the front door was equally blocked by heavy furniture. Several people appeared from their various hiding positions around the home. He knew without her having to say a word that she'd rounded up those she could, then after barricading the house, stood guard while they hid in the bedrooms of her home. He flicked his gaze around the kitchen. The table was covered with guns and clips of ammo. Jake guessed the reason the men had been hiding was because once they'd shot out the windows, his mate gave them a taste of their own medicine. As horrific as this attack on her home had been, she'd stayed strong and saved others. Jake couldn't help but be proud of her. She was one hundred percent a true alpha mate.

Stroking his palms over Sophie, he forced his mind back to the present.

"I just got off the phone to Jessie. He told me a man attempted to snatch Kit from a checkpoint at the rally today. Jessie arrived as Kit was freeing herself so only caught a glimpse of the guy, but he saw eye logos on his shirt."

He loved Kit like he did his sons. She was part of his family and the thought of someone taking her, especially Trigger, seared his soul. After they helped bury the dead and cover up what had happened in her hometown, Sophie had returned to Rosebery with Jake. He'd attempted to convince his father to research Trigger, but his father had told him to leave it alone. He knew enough about Trigger to know that the last thing they needed was to attract their attention to their leap. He had confided that one of the reasons the Continental leap was based in Tasmania was due to the fact that most of the mainland,

and the world at large, didn't worry about what happened down here. But Jake wondered if maybe it was now time to do some more research into them. For the most part, all the global Continental leaps were preoccupied with finding lost ones; large scale massacres by Trigger were extremely rare, so as a whole they'd grown complacent. The Continental leap alphas had all concluded long ago it was more important to find their missing than go looking for trouble from a bloodthirsty cult. But now, with them coming after his own, Jake was wondering if that priority shouldn't change.

Sophie lifted her head and locked her gaze with his. The look in her eye told him she'd been deep in thought.

"Jake, honey, we don't know all of Kit's past. She's never confided in us her birth name. Remember back to when we found her? That sweet little kitten was so scared of everything, nearly starved to death as she roamed the mountains in her new leopard form, yet she still refused to go back to her home. Surely, if she'd simply been told to get out, she would have attempted to go back. But she didn't. She's never wanted to, even as an adult. It may not be Trigger. Plenty of companies use logos that at a glance look like an eye, and it was only one man. The little we know of Trigger, they send gangs or at least a pair, not individuals. Especially after someone like Kit; any fool can see she's trained and in no way an easy target. So far we've stayed safe from them here in Tasmania. They haven't bothered with crossing Bass Strait before, so why now?"

He continued to run his hands over his mate's back and through her soft hair as he took some deep breaths. Sophie was right of course.

"I hope I am jumping to conclusions, love. But I can feel it in my gut that something's coming. Something evil." He paused on a sigh, "Maybe we shouldn't have allowed Kit her privacy. I could have gone digging to find more information on her."

She leaned up and stroked her fingertips over the contours of his face, her touch calming his racing mind as it always did.

"Maybe. But that's in the past. We can't do anything to change it. Just promise me that you'll research this before you start panicking everyone, okay? I'm not saying it's not them. Trust me, I hope and pray it's not Trigger, but they are bound to find us eventually. They appear to find every leap at some point."

"They seem to. Okay, I need to ring the Alpha Council and see if anyone else has seen an increase in Trigger activity lately."

He kissed his wife and mate soundly on the lips, putting all the love he felt for her into it, before he stood and allowed her to lead him to their bedroom. He'd shredded his clothes when he'd shifted earlier and he needed to get dressed before he started work.

Kit sipped her beer as she sat across from Jessie. This all felt so normal, so human. She chuckled to herself. Her first date and she was drinking beer while basically hiding in the back of a hotel restaurant. Maybe they should complete the cliché and start necking?

Jessie cocked his head a little. "Why you laughing like that?"

"Just thinking if we start groping each other and pashing we'd have the whole first date cliché down pat."

A slight frown marred his features. "Pashing?"

"You know? Making out, kissing, snogging…"

"Ahh, okay. Another Australian slang word. I don't think this table is secluded enough to get away with that, so we'll have to save the groping and pashing for later," he finished with a wink.

Her stomach tightened when his eyes suddenly turned serious as he reached for her hand that rested on the table. "Kit, who came after you today?"

In one last ditch effort to avoid this conversation, she answered with a half truth, "Never seen the guy before."

"Yeah, well, the way you just screwed up your face tells me you might not know him personally, but you've got a fair idea who sent him."

With a little huff, she mentally shook her head. Of course Jessie wasn't going to let this go. He was a shifter and someone had come after his mate. She was going to have to be completely honest with him. With a wince, she dropped her gaze to their joined hands. His skin was slightly darker than hers. Damn, her smaller hand did look good with his larger one wrapped around it.

"I recognized the logo on his shirt."

"The eye?"

"You saw it too, huh? Well, next time you see it have a close look. It's actually not an eye at all. It's the trigger of a rifle. They've tricked it up a bit so it looks less obvious."

"Considering that Jake told me to stay far away from anyone wearing that logo, I'll pass on taking a closer look and just take your word for it."

A rush of panic filled her and she squeezed his hand while holding his gaze. "I wasn't telling you to go after someone wearing the thing! I was thinking more along the lines of you doing a Google search. I would never, *ever* send anyone after that bunch of thugs."

"You're talking like you know more than Jake does. He couldn't tell me much other than to stay away and don't attract their attention."

Damn it, how much did she reveal to him? "I don't know a whole heap either. I didn't want to set off any red flags by searching too deep. I know before Jake and Sophie found me, they attempted to trap me. I heard them say they thought it would be a piece of cake to catch such a young leopard, and that their boss would be happy to have such a specimen. As you can imagine, I didn't hang around."

"After I got off the phone to Jake I did a little googling. I found references to them being a research based company and also noticed them mentioned in regard to a couple of gang attacks back in the eighties."

"Yeah, I found the same things. Those gang attacks were on leaps. Jake's mate, Sophie is from Broome." She paused as he frowned; of course he wouldn't know where that was. "Upper northwest corner of Australia. Her leap was all but destroyed by a Trigger gang. Only a handful survived. Choden told me about it once. He knew I was looking into them and he warned me not to bring their attention to Rosebery. He told me Jake's father, the then alpha, sent Jake and a few strong shifters up there to help them after Jake dream bonded with Sophie and she begged him to help her. They nearly arrived too late. Sophie had a small group stashed in a house that was surrounded by Trigger. Jake and his boys cleared them out and rescued them but the rest of the leap had been slaughtered."

"But that guy this morning was alone, wasn't he?"

"Yeah, and I don't get that. As far as I've been able to find, they don't act alone. Did he just stumble across me and on a whim decide to take me out? Maybe they're not here at all, and it's simply a member that happens to be holidaying down here or something. I'm not sure but it will pay to keep an eye out for them, and try to never be alone."

A waitress brought over their meals and that thankfully ended the conversation. Kit didn't want to think about Trigger more than she had to. Without another word, Kit settled into eating her meal. When she was about halfway through, Jessie obviously decided he didn't like the comfortable silence she'd been enjoying.

"So, you live around here?"

Grateful for a safer topic, Kit swallowed her mouthful

and answered, "I could never live here in Hobart. Too many people. I live in Rosebery."

"That near where your friend was attacked?"

She winced a little at the reminder, so much for a safer topic. Trigger weren't the only ones out to hurt her and her kind. She needed to ring Conner or Tina and find out how she was going. Maybe she should call Sophie. No doubt Conner and Tina weren't feeling like socializing yet. Although, Jessie had obviously rung Jake and told him about Trigger, no doubt Jake was in full panic mode right about now, so Sophie would be busy.

"Ah, yeah. Just down the road. Tina was taken to the Rosebery Hospital."

"Your parents live there too?"

She clenched her fork as anger flashed through her system. On top of the Trigger shit, she did not want to even think about her parents, let alone talk of them.

"No. I live on my own."

She held his gaze as she spoke, making it clear it was not up for discussion. She saw pain flicker in their depths before he lowered his head and took another bite of his dinner. Her appetite had evaporated. The very thought of her parents always had that effect. With a huff, she pushed her plate aside and took a deep swallow of her beer.

"Please, Kit, eat some more. I'm sorry if my question upset you. I'm just trying to get to know you better, that's all."

Kit sat straighter as anger coursed through her. How

dare he want her to reveal her gritty past when he'd shared nothing about his with her?

"Well, you could start with something about you. You've told me nothing, yet you want me to spill."

"Start eating and I'll tell you... Something."

Frowning, she watched him closely as she took another mouthful of beer. Would it be that easy to get Jessie to open up? She took her time placing the drink back down. What to do… In the end curiosity won out, and she had nothing to lose by eating. She pulled her plate back in front of her and took a mouthful. As she chewed, he carefully set his cutlery down and wiped his mouth, clearly deep in thought.

"I grew up in Arica, which is at the northern end of Chile. My father was a businessman, not real sure what business he was in. He was a bastard who seemed to only come home to drink and knock my mama and me around. My mama was a beautiful and gentle woman. She was my whole world and I was devastated when she passed away two years ago after having a massive heart attack.

"My childhood was spent in a middle class area. We had just enough and were lucky to have a decent house. Then, after…" He paused on a wince and reached for his beer to take a deep drink, and Kit took another mouthful of food. She wasn't hungry and barely tasted the food but she didn't want Jessie to stop, so she kept eating. "After my fifteenth birthday, it was just me and Mama. We had to leave the home we'd been in, so we moved to a house with another two families. It was hard but at least I didn't have to watch my mama get beaten every other day. I'd already been hanging out with a friend of my mama's, Carlos, at his garage before we moved. I loved cars, everything about them. How they sounded, how they worked. Carlos took me under his wing after what happened. One thing led to another and I got into rallying."

Kit's mind spun with questions and she put her fork down. What had happened to him after he'd shifted that first time?

"What happened to your dad?"

Fire flared in his eyes. "I don't know you nearly well enough to discuss that. I just told you more than most people, even my teammates, know about me. Please, Kit, don't ask for more than I can give."

She huffed out a breath and forced herself to eat another mouthful, as she needed a moment or two. What could she tell him?

"I grew up in Wollongong, which is down the coast from Sydney. Average childhood, my dad's a police detective, mum's a housewife, at least they were. I assume it hasn't changed. They emigrated from Chile when I was just a baby. They never had any other kids. Not sure what else to tell you. I wasn't the most popular kid in school, but I had a number of friends. I was happy, with nothing really to complain about. Well, not until I turned fifteen. I banged around a bit when I shifted that first time and they came running. Then they kicked me out."

She stopped to take a drink. Why was she telling Jessie this shit? She'd never told anyone what happened that morning. Not even Jake or Sophie knew it all. And Jessie had not trusted her with what had happened after his first shift. Swallowing the last of her beer, she rose from her seat.

"Want another drink?"

"They'll come to us, Kit."

"Eventually. I need another drink now. You want one or not?"

"Yeah, thanks."

She hightailed it over to the bar and ordered two more beers. Fuck, what was she doing? Even though he was her mate, he hadn't given her any indicators that he wanted to stick around after the rally. What would she do if he left her? Jake had told her that because they were mates, he wouldn't be able to stand being parted from her, but she couldn't quite bring herself to believe it was going to be that simple.

Gabriel re-read the email. He'd asked an old buddy who was on the force to keep an eye on any reports that came in regarding the rally. So far he'd proved most useful. Gabriel needed to know when crap like this went down.

Bill was such a fucking fool. Did he seriously think he could simply grab the redhead? No adult shifter was an easy mark, especially not one who was skilled as she was. From seeing her fight, he knew she'd been well trained.

When he heard a car pull up to their rental house he calmly shut down his computer. Gabriel was going to have a little chat with young Bill. He stood from his seat and began to roll up the sleeves of his button-down shirt. The front door slowly swung open with a small squeak as Bill attempted to slip silently inside. Stupid fool was wearing a Trigger shirt too. Damn, Gabriel hoped Bill hadn't been spotted by anyone who knew what that logo meant. In any case, they were going to have to lay low for a few days to avoid raising suspicions.

"Busy morning, Bill?"

He ran his gaze over the man, noticing his reddened cheek, which was already bruising. Bill was also cradling his right hand with his left. So, only two obvious injuries. Gabriel was almost disappointed. He'd thought the redhead would have done more damage.

"Not overly, just went and scoped out the rally for a while."

Gabriel crossed his arms over his chest as he quirked a brow. "And you what? Tripped over a shifter and landed on your cheek?"

Bill dropped his hands and clenched them into fists as his gaze hardened and he stormed over to stand in front of Gabriel.

"You know already. Your little fucking spy's reported in, hasn't he?"

Gabriel could see Bill's chest heaving with his anger. The young man was so susceptible to letting his emotions over take him.

"Yes, I know how you attacked the redhead. Be thankful she chose to not chase you down or lay charges. I am curious as to the reason behind you assaulting her. We're only meant to be watching at the moment, we're only to capture ones that are easy marks. She was never going to be an easy mark."

"Yeah, well, she's a real fucking easy distraction for you. You want to nail her or some shit? Because ever since we arrived, you've been solely focused on her. I'm the only one looking elsewhere for more shifters. You, buddy, have tunnel vision bad when it comes to that female and it's gonna cost us both our lives if we don't watch it. All I was doing was trying to remove a distraction."

Fury clouded Gabriel's mind. This fool thought Gabriel needed a caretaker while on a job? It was beyond insulting. In a sharp, fast movement, Gabriel thrust a hand into Bill's shirt, taking a firm grip of the loose material.

"You are not my minder, boy. I am the superior officer. It is me that monitors you, not the other way around. If I so much as get a hint of you going after the redhead on your own I will put you in the ground. Do you understand me?"

The cocky little shit didn't back down. "You sure about that, old man?"

Before Gabriel realized what he'd done, he heard the crunch of bone as pain flared in his knuckles. Bill was fast. Ignoring his obviously broken nose, he swung a fast haymaker punch at Gabriel's head. Releasing Bill's shirt, Gabriel blocked the shot, took hold of his wrist and pulled it back, spinning the fool around so his arm was pinned up behind his back. In a move faster than he'd thought Bill capable of, he kicked back, landing a blow against the side of Gabriel's knee, forcing that leg to buckle and drop him down. With a curse, Gabriel sprung to his feet just in time to block another shot to his face. A second punch landed against his ribs before he could do anything about it.

"You just don't learn do you, boy? I am the boss here. Not you. Never you."

Shifting his weight, he put his whole body behind a roundhouse kick that knocked Bill flat on his back, fortunately, missing the coffee table. He didn't need to be ringing the higher-ups and explaining how furniture got broken.

"Do you understand what I'm saying to you yet?"

"For fucks sake, Gabriel! Look at yourself. You're obsessed with her, and it's not healthy. Fine, you don't want me going after her. She'll stay on the list to be taken down when backup arrives. But she will go down. She's too dangerous to be left roaming around freely and you know it. And now she's on that takedown list, we don't need to watch her every damn move."

Bill slowly dragged himself up off the floor. "And if you ever touch me again, I'll come after you when you least expect it and take you down. Understand *me*? There are reasons I was recruited. I'm not some meek, mild accountant type. Just you remember that, old man."

He walked away toward the bedrooms mumbling some shit about the fact he needed to start carrying a blade again and fuck the police and their laws that said he couldn't.

Gabriel wasn't sure how long he stood there. *Fuck.* If Bill had caught on to his little obsession, had word got back to the higher-ups? Surely he could just explain how dangerous she was and that was why he was watching her closely. Yeah, they would understand that reasoning.

He took a deep breath and winced. Damn little punk could land a punch. His ribs would be stinging for a while. He followed Bill's path and headed to his own bedroom where he stripped down and made his way to the bathroom. He'd never been so grateful this place had two of them so he didn't have to share with the little bastard.

Chapter Five

Jessie entered his room to find Pedro waiting up for him. The TV played in the background with the volume down low, but Pedro's attention was now fully focused on Jessie.

"You're back early. Didn't expect to see you till morning to be honest."

"So why you waiting up for me then?"

"Okay, let me rephrase. I'd hoped you wouldn't be back till morning, but I suspected you'd be back tonight. Way too early."

"Tonight was never going to end that way, *amigo*. Tomorrow's the final day of racing. I need to have a good night's sleep to be ready. Kit understands that. Tonight was only ever going to be simply dinner and getting to know each other."

And shit, the little he'd learned...it wasn't nearly enough. When she'd come back from the bar, she'd not uttered another word about her childhood. Jessie desperately wanted to know what had happened to her after she'd been kicked out following her first shift. But he suspected the only way she'd spill that information was if he told her something more of himself too. And he wasn't ready to do that. He'd already told her more than he'd intended to. Maybe it was the whole mate thing that seemed to mess with his ability to filter his speech.

"I'm going to hit the shower then head to bed."

He hurried to lock himself in the bathroom before Pedro could respond. The damn man knew him too well and often saw things Jessie wished he didn't. As he stepped under the warm rush of water, he pondered what Jake had said to him about Kit needing him, but he couldn't see how he'd fit in to her life. She really didn't need a man and Jessie didn't like the idea of becoming some woman's shadow, following her around, hoping she'd need him one day. If he was going to enter into a serious relationship with a woman, he had to know he was an essential part of her life. He was also caveman enough that he wanted to be the protector of his woman.

With a sigh, he put his face under the warm spray. Tomorrow night there was a huge black tie ball, then the rally would officially be over and he'd have no reason to stay in Tasmania. What the hell was he meant to do? With his mama gone, he didn't have any family left in Chile and only had a couple of friends. Pedro, likewise, didn't have much waiting for him back home. Hell, he'd probably love to join Jessie in moving Down Under.

Fifteen minutes later he left the bathroom to find Pedro had fallen asleep with the TV still going. He flicked the machine off and slid into his own bed. The cool crisp sheets felt nice against his skin heated from the hot shower. As he got comfortable, an image of Kit from earlier in the night filled his mind. She was chuckling between taking sips of her beer. She was so damn beautiful, especially when she'd leaned back to drink and bared her throat. Jessie wanted her. He couldn't deny it. But she was a virgin. A beautiful innocent virgin, who deserved better than a murdering animal like him.

With those thoughts running through his mind, he wasn't overly surprised to discover that when he slipped into sleep, he was instantly dreaming of her, but not as she was now. In his dream, she was much younger, still in her teens.

He sat on a train filled with people dressed for work. Business suits surrounded him. Where was he? He looked up at the advertisements attached to the walls of the carriage, trying to find something to give him an idea. A large poster that read "Bring in 2002 with a bang at Sydney Harbor" spanned the space above the automatic doors. Right. Sydney, Australia. Ten years ago. Was Kit here? He focused back on the bustling carriage and started searching. Was her red hair natural? Or would she have another color? For that matter, was this his dream or hers? If it was his, he had no idea why he'd be dreaming of a city he'd never visited. This whole dream bonding thing was more than a little spooky. Maybe because he'd been thinking of her as he'd fallen asleep he pushed himself into her dream?

He caught a flash of red up the other end of the carriage and began to push his way through all the people to get to her. When he caught a glimpse of her face, he stopped his approach. She had her feet up on her seat with her legs folded up tightly against her chest. Her arms were wrapped around them as her cheek rested on the top of her knees. Her eyes were rimmed red, as if she'd be crying, and she had a backpack looped over one of her shoulders so it sat next to her. She looked like she'd dressed in a hurry, or maybe in a daze. The laces on her sneakers were undone, and her shirt looked all pulled out of whack. With a little sigh that ripped into his heart, she moved to rub her eyes on her jean-clad knees. He wanted nothing more than to go to her, to gather her up and comfort her, but he didn't know how it would affect the dream. Nor was he sure if Kit would recognize him in the dream. Was she the adult Kit in her younger body or fully her younger self?

Eventually the train began to stop and start with regularity as the buildings outside rose higher. Looking out at the sky, he guessed it was early morning. There weren't any school kids on the train so he assumed it was maybe around seven. When they were in the inner city, Kit rose from her seat and slipped out the door. Jessie rushed to follow her, having to push past several people to make it to the doors before they closed.

He followed her as she seemed to aimlessly amble around the city. What was she doing? Finally, after what felt like hours, he decided to call out to her.

"Kit?"

She didn't respond, didn't slow her stride. He frowned in thought. Couldn't she see him? He rubbed a hand over the back of his neck. He really needed to have a long chat with Jake about all the crap that came with these dreams. With nothing else to do and with no idea how to leave the dream, he continued to follow her. She stopped in a couple of parks, curling up on the grass in the sun for a while before she rose and moved on. As the sky darkened, she began to head toward less populated parts of the city. Damn, poverty looked the same no matter where it was. The rough houses, dirty streets and homeless settling down on the sidewalks were all too familiar from his own teen years.

She stiffened as a group of older boys came down the street. She held her head high but her eyes showed her fear. And naturally, these thugs saw it. All four of them circled her, stopping her forward movement.

"Whatcha doing, girlie?"

"Yeah, where you going?"

"Looking for a good time are ya?"

The sly comments kept coming at her. Jessie had hung back, still unsure whether he could make a difference to anything that happened in the dream. But if these bastards tried to hurt her, he'd test the theory in an attempt to protect her. Jessie couldn't stand the thought of her being injured.

He stepped forward as one reached out and touched her hair, pulling a chunk of the red through his fingers.

"Such a pretty little thing to be out on her own."

She slapped his hand away and that set the wheels in motion. With a curse, the thug went to backhand her. Kit sunk back into a fighter's stance as she blocked the blow and delivered one of her own to his face. With a howl, he spun away from her. The other three seemed to be stunned still for a moment but it didn't last long and soon they closed in on her.

Jessie watched a little in shock and a lot in awe as Kit kicked and punched her way free of them. They kept coming at her and she kept blocking and hitting back. After she landed that first punch, the thugs were a little more careful, blocking what they could. Occasionally Kit was taking a hit but she took them with barely a flinch. Who the hell had trained her? At fifteen she had a skill level he'd not seen often in adults.

Even with her expertise, four onto one was far from a fair fight and eventually one got a grip on her. Jessie admired her guts. She refused to go down. The thug held her from behind and she quickly took her arms from her backpack to get free. She spun, and with a low kick took out his legs. He hit the ground with a curse but was soon back up. He looked down at the bag on the ground with sly grin.

"Well, guess since we can't take you, we'll just have to take your stuff, huh, girlie?"

He snatched up her bag and ran, his buddies following his lead. With a cry, Kit took off after them, but she was obviously tired from the fight and she soon lost them. Puffed, she stopped and lowered her head. She braced her hands on her knees as she leaned forward and took deep breaths. Kit was breaking his heart. This was obviously the day after her first shift. He wanted to try again to approach her but before he could touch her, she stood straight and began walking again. She didn't stop until she reached a park. Confused, Jessie followed. What was she up to? She had purpose in her stride.

She walked right up to a tree and jumped to grip the lower branch. With a couple of quick movements, she swung up into the branches and proceeded to climb higher into the foliage that hid her presence. Once she found a spot where she could secure herself, she curled up and closed her eyes. Jessie could see the tears that ran down her cheeks as they reflected the moonlight. He rubbed at the ache in his chest before a wind picked up and colors swirled around him as he left the park and another place began to form.

Caught between her past and the present, Kit huddled up in the tree. She knew Jessie was down below. He'd been silently watching her relive this hellish day. He'd called out to her once and she'd desperately wanted to acknowledge him, to let him stop the progression of memories but she couldn't derail her younger self from following the events of that day.

Unsure if Jessie would follow her, she pulled free from the memory and reformed in a large clearing high in the Cradle Mountains. She opened her eyes from her adult body and saw Jessie standing in front of her. The sympathy in his gaze set her teeth on edge and made her lash out.

"How dare you invade my dream without permission?"

He raised his hands in front of him. "I didn't mean to, Kit. I have no idea how any of this shit works."

"It's real simple. You think of me as you're falling asleep, you enter my dream. Unless you're focused on wanting to meet somewhere specific, then you call me to you."

Jessie stayed silent. The anger in his eyes faded as he cocked his head to the side and folded his arms over his chest.

"You done yelling at me?"

She growled at him for seeing through her defenses. How dare he!

"No one knows about that day. No. One. I've never told a single soul about what happened before I came to Rosebery. It's no one's business but mine."

"Yeah, I get that, Kit. Trust me, what happened after my first shift was arguably worse."

Damn, she wanted to hit him! His was worse? Gah, did all men have to be so damn selfish? Even pain, they had to do one better.

"How could it have been worse? I was kicked out. Told by my father, the man I idolized and looked up to, that if he ever saw me again he'd kill me. I had one chance so I had better make it count. Then, as you saw, I caught the train into the big city, hoping to find a shelter or something that would take me in, but all I found was thieves and thugs. So I took a train out to the Blue

Mountains, figured life as a snow leopard would have to be better. Turns out I was wrong. I didn't know how to hunt, and I struggled to stay hidden. If Jake and Sophie hadn't come for me when they did, I'd have been dead soon after."

Jessie's silver blue irises had turned to ice as he held her stare. "You truly want to know how mine could be worse?"

The look in his eyes gave her pause. What the fuck had happened to him? Suddenly proving who had it worse wasn't important. Finding out everything she could about him was. She felt the heat of her fury seep from her body. Her shoulders sagged as her body relaxed a little.

"Please, Jessie. But not because I want to trade whose fifteenth birthday sucked more. I want to know something about you that I can't find out online along with every other rally groupie. Please trust me, Jessie."

She stayed silent, praying he'd give in and tell her while he clenched and unclenched his jaw a number of times before taking a deep breath.

"I murdered my father."

Her hand flew to her mouth in shock. That was definitely not what she'd expected him to say.

"Yeah, you heard right. The morning after my change, my mama found me, naked and scared on my bedroom floor. She'd thought I was sick and wanted me to tell her what was wrong. So I showed her what I could now do. Then my father came in. First, he accused Mama of being unfaithful. But I look just like the bastard, so there was

never any doubt about who fathered me. Not to mention my mother would never do such a thing. His next accusation was that one of us had been messing with black magic. He hit both of us before he turned all his attention on beating my mama. With how mad he was, I knew he was going to kill her this time." He paused as he shrugged his shoulders. "I followed my instincts."

Kit didn't know what to say. She didn't know what to think. She took a step toward him and when he didn't back away she went all the way to him and wrapped her arms around his waist. After a moment, his hands slid up her back and she felt his cheek against the side of her temple.

"No one else knows what happened that night. Mama helped me clean up and took me out for a birthday breakfast. When we returned home, she rang the police. It was clearly an animal attack. I think Pedro suspects what happened that morning as he knows what I am. But that's it."

"I'm sorry."

What else could she say? Damn, between the two of them they had more baggage than a bloody airline.

"Don't be. It wasn't your fault. There are days when I still struggle with the guilt, but thinking about the long, happy life my mama had afterward, not being beaten every other day, helps ease it."

Kit wasn't sure how to continue and after a few minutes of awkward silence, she decided on a complete subject change.

"So, one more day of racing left. How are your times looking?"

His arms tightened and he pressed a kiss to her forehead. "Smooth topic change, reinita. *My times are good but I doubt I'll be up on the podium tomorrow."*

"Guess I'll see you during the day, like usual."

"You want to go to the black tie gala as my date?"

She smiled as she pressed her face closer to his throat, breathing in his clean, masculine scent. "You just want to see me in a dress."

"Well, that's certainly a factor. Tell me, do you own one, or will you need to go shopping tomorrow?"

With a chuckle, she pulled from his embrace. She gave him a light tap on the chest. "I own plenty of dresses, Jessie. Well, at least a couple. Maybe."

Kit was sure there was at least one somewhere in her wardrobe that wasn't a bridesmaid dress. Jessie gave her a wide cheeky grin. "Well, with that to look forward to I may just race fast enough to get on that podium tomorrow."

The entire day had been one big blur as Jessie couldn't wait to see what Kit would look like in a dress. He bet she'd spent today shopping for it, despite what she'd told him.

"So, Jessie. Racing's all done for the season... You made up your mind about what you're going to do yet?"

Jessie focused on his reflection in the mirror as he popped his collar up and wrapped the strip of black material around his neck. Not wanting to answer Pedro's question, he pretended to be totally engrossed as he tied his bow tie just like Carlos had shown him years ago. As he smoothed down his collar, he realized he was out of things to do in the bathroom. His hair was slicked back, and his teeth brushed. With a sigh, he turned to face his friend.

"I honestly don't know, Pedro. I mean, I have to go back initially, but whether I'll stay there or return here to be with Kit. I'm not sure."

"*Amigo*, you know as well as I do that you could stay. If your mama was here she'd tell you to follow your heart and move forward with life. I'll soon pack up your stuff and ship it over. Hell, I might even move over here with you. Assuming we'd both be able to get immigration to let us."

Jessie closed his eyes as he rubbed the bridge of his nose. His mind was a mess when it came to anything to do with Kit. What he needed was more time. Part of him didn't want to leave at all. It refused the very concept of leaving Kit's side, and he was very tempted by Pedro's offer. Yet, another larger portion of him was still convinced he didn't deserve her. Even though she was a strong woman and had been through a lot, she remained innocent and pure. So Jessie was caught between worrying she didn't need him as she continually proved she was more than capable of taking care of herself, and that if he touched her he'd taint her purity with his roughness.

"I can't make a forever kind of decision after a couple of days, Pedro."

"Well, we fly out tomorrow. You don't have the luxury of more time."

Yeah, he knew exactly when they were leaving. His team manager was sending him and Pedro home earlier than usual, leaving the pack up to the rest of the crew. He'd tried to argue it when he'd found out, but Luan had insisted. But then Luan knew that in two days' time it was the anniversary of his mother's death. Knew that Jessie would want to be able to leave her flowers and have some alone time. Luan was good like that and always made sure he knew everything he could about everyone on the team.

"All I know at this point is that I'll be on that plane tomorrow. I have to go visit Mama the day after we land. Then? Who knows…"

Pedro didn't respond, just squeezed Jessie's shoulder on his way out the door. Jessie followed him down to the lobby where he'd arranged to meet Kit before they headed into the function room, which was all decked out for the gala. With his heart in his throat, he looked around the crowded room for her but he couldn't see her. A cool breeze carrying her scent reached him, and he turned toward the front door. She must have gone home or to a friend's place to get ready, as Jessie knew she had a room here at the hotel.

As he took in the sight of her, he forgot how to breathe. Kit was a vision. Her trim, athletic body was encased in a stunning emerald green gown. The strapless top showed off her perfectly smooth, tanned shoulders. Jessie licked his lips at the sight of the swells of her breasts above that delicate fabric wrapped around her. The dress clung tightly to the seductive curve of her waist and as she stepped forward, a split in the long skirt revealed her incredibly well-toned sexy legs, from her thigh down to her stiletto heels.

He couldn't help but grin at the slightly pinched look on her face. She was nervous. Jessie moved toward her and growled quietly when he noticed all the male attention she was receiving. It seemed as if every man in the place was watching her, except for the two she'd walked in with. The twins she'd worked the rally with stood guard on either side of her. They aimed feral looks at any male who attempted to approach her. Kit's gaze roamed the crowd and when she saw him, she blushed a little before glancing down. *She is so damn sweet and innocent*. Especially at times like this when she was outside her comfort zone. He pushed his way through the crowd to get to her.

"*Hola reinita*, you look amazing in that gown."

"Oh, this old thing? I just threw it on. You don't scrub up so bad yourself."

The twins tried to hold her back from him, but she glared at each of them as she pushed past them.

"Back it up, boys. Jessie is my mate, not some random bloke trying to grab a feel. I'll catch you both later."

Jessie was a little surprised they retreated so easily.

They knew who he was from that first day they'd met, and they also knew his reputation. He couldn't imagine they'd be happy about him being with their leap sister. When she was standing before him, he reached out and allowed the small section of hair she'd left hanging over her face to glide between his finger and thumb. The rest of her red waves were pinned up in a fancy style that was both elegant and alluring.

"So very pretty, Kit."

A light blush covered her cheeks once more, and Jessie decided he liked the look on her, even though it made her appear even younger and more innocent.

"Yeah, well, it's a black tie gala. I didn't think they'd let me in wearing my bike leathers or my firefighting gear."

She was nervously chatting and it was so damn cute. With her like this, all soft and feminine, he couldn't stand the thought of leaving her tomorrow. What the hell was he meant to do?

"Come on, *reinita.* Let's grab a drink and find a table."

Sipping at her wine, Kit relaxed as much as she could into the stiff-backed chair. She'd been so damn nervous wearing this dress. She'd gone shopping with Adele and Tina this morning to get it and had to admit that even she could see that the emerald color contrasted very nicely with her red hair. Obviously, she hadn't been able to ride her bike in this getup so she arranged to catch a lift with the twins from Adele's place to the hotel. When Joel and

Jordan had rocked up, they'd cursed before proclaiming themselves her bodyguards for the evening. Apparently, with her looking so good they were going to have to spend their night batting away drooling men. She'd laughed them off until they'd arrived. From the moment she stepped from the car, she'd had males trying to paw her. Turned out she'd needed bloody bodyguards, at least until she was beside Jessie. Once she had her arm wrapped around his, the other men seemed to accept she was unavailable and were content to stand back and drool. She'd still felt their gazes on her, but thankfully they didn't attempt to approach her anymore.

Now, the gala was winding down as she sat with Jessie surrounded by the rest of his team. The conversation had been light and slightly comical. These guys didn't forget a thing and had told Kit every embarrassing tidbit they could about Jessie. Man, some of the shit he'd done. Kit was grateful to them for keeping the stories clean and not mentioning any of the women Jessie had messed around with.

With one more swallow of wine, her glass was empty and she leaned forward to place it on the table. She misjudged and nearly knocked it over. Damn, how much had she drunk? Thinking back she couldn't quite remember. The waiters had been very good at their jobs, keeping her glass full. She guessed now things were nearly over they'd stopped that service for the night so she'd finally reached the bottom of her glass.

"You okay, *reinita*?"

"Yeah, just a little tipsy. What does that mean anyway?"

"What? *Reinita*?"

"That's the one. Is it Spanish?"

"It's a term of endearment we say in Chile, basically means 'princess'."

Kit screwed her nose up. "I'm hardly a princess, Jessie."

A gasp left her throat as he pulled her from her seat onto his lap.

"To me, you are my *reinita*. Precious and to be cherished."

Chuckling at his comment, she leaned into him. Between the alcohol buzzing through her system and his scent filling her senses, she was flying high and perfectly happy about it.

"*Chucha*, you two. Get a room!"

Pedro's comment had her face heating as she pulled back from Jessie. Crap, she'd basically forgotten they were in public.

"That sounds like a great idea, Pedro. The awards are all finished with now and since I didn't get a podium place, they don't need me for photos or anything else. I'm all for moving this party to a room."

Pedro laughed in response to Jessie's slightly slurred speech.

"Guess I'll find somewhere else to bunk down tonight, *amigo*."

Kit shook her head, "No, Pedro. The room's all yours.

I have my own room, we can go there."

The entire table started laughing, and Kit felt her face go flame hot as she realized what she'd just said. She groaned as she buried her face against Jessie's neck.

"Don't worry, Kit. They're just jealous they don't have a sexy kitten purring in their laps."

She didn't think that was the case, but she appreciated him trying to make her feel better.

"Yeah, Kit, cause you know everybody wants a woman like Jessie's girl."

Kit groaned as they all started singing Rick Springfield's song, "Jessie's Girl." Without another word, she hopped off Jessie's lap and grabbed his hand. As fast as she could in her heels, she led Jessie from the room while she vainly tried to block out the singing. Damn it, if any of her leap brothers were still here, she'd never live this one down. Fortunately there weren't many people hanging around the lobby so they got to the elevator quickly.

The ride up was silent as they weren't alone. Jessie tugged her against him, so her back was pressed up to his chest, and he wrapped his arms around her waist. He leaned down and whispered in her ear.

"I like this dress. Standing like this I have a stunning view."

She looked down and sure enough, Jessie had a clear view down her cleavage. *Gah, men!* She gave him a soft jab with her elbow as the doors opened and she walked clear of the elevator. As she made her way down the hallway, some of the alcohol haze cleared as nerves crept in. She was a virgin and Jessie wasn't. He was experienced with these things. Would she disappoint him?

Jessie followed her into her room. As the door shut with a soft click, she turned to face him. Unsure what to do, Kit stood still clenching and unclenching her hands into fists to vent her nervous energy. Jessie stripped out of his jacket and tossed it over the back of a chair. He loosened his bow tie as he prowled toward her. Kit chewed on her lower lip at the sight he made. With an alpha male's confidence, he didn't stop until he was toe to toe with her.

As he gripped the back of her neck with a large palm, she had a fleeting thought that they really should discuss the future beyond tomorrow before they went any further. When he pulled her to him on a low growl and took her mouth with his, her mind cleared of everything but her lust for Jessie. She tentatively ran her hands up his chest, feeling his hard muscles bunch beneath the thin cotton of his shirt. Her nails dug into his shoulders as his hand that wasn't holding her neck, ran down her spine, taking her zipper with it.

As he feathered kisses from her mouth down over her jaw, he ran his fingers from her neck up into her hair. She felt the pins fall free and her hair brush against her bare back. He kissed his way down her throat before he pulled away from her body. Under the intensity of his heated stare, she shuddered, which caused her dress to fall from her body to land in a heap around her feet.

Chapter Six

Jessie hissed in a breath as Kit's naked body was revealed. She was exquisite. Total perfection. His already aroused body hardened further. His erection strained against his pants, desperate to get to her. He clenched his jaw and took a deep breath. He needed to go slowly, so he had to tamp down his fierce desire for her.

"So beautiful."

Restraining his need to devour her, he lightly ran a fingertip over the soft skin of her shoulder and down to her lush breast where he circled her nipple, groaning a little as it tightened and hardened for him.

"You're wearing too many clothes, Jessie."

His lips quirked at her breathy voice before he once again took her mouth in a searing kiss. Why couldn't they be able to magic away their clothes like shifters do in the movies? Jessie wanted to be naked with her but didn't want to release his hold on her to do it. Reluctantly, he stepped away from the temptation of her body. After undoing the top few buttons on his shirt, he lost patience and ripped the thing over his head and tossed it aside. He didn't care one bit that buttons had pinged from it, probably wrecking the shirt. With fast movements, he slipped his belt off and undid his fly, his fingers fumbling in his haste, and he paused when Kit stepped from the puddle of material surrounding her feet. Every movement she made was smooth and graceful and sent all his blood straight to his dick. The thing was throbbing now. He'd never been this aroused before. In this moment, with his body humming with desire for her, none of his previous doubts mattered. Standing in front of him bare and open to him, she raised an eyebrow at him as she eyed his hands frozen in the process of taking off his pants. He mentally shook free from his thoughts. He needed to be naked to make Kit his. The need to have her under him was becoming all-consuming. If he didn't hurry up, he'd be so desperate for her he'd lose his ability to take her slowly. She was a virgin and the last thing Jessie wanted was to hurt her more than absolutely necessary.

Toeing off his shoes, he quickly shucked his pants and boxers in one movement. He pulled a condom from his wallet and tossed it onto the bedside cupboard. Part of him wanted to take her with nothing between them, but he couldn't do that. He wouldn't take Kit without protection unless they were fully committed to one another. He'd never once had sex without a condom. He didn't want to risk fathering a child with a woman he didn't want to spend the rest of his life with. Nor had he wanted to risk passing on his genetics.

Stroking himself, he ran his gaze from Kit's delicate toes all the way to the fiery curls surrounding her face.

He smirked at her expression. Her lips were parted and her eyes wide. She watched him palm himself with what appeared to be a mix of shock and awe. *You know how to boost a man's ego, reinita.* Releasing his hold on himself, Jessie prowled over to where she stood a few steps away. He knew he was well hung and she, understandably, had doubts as to how he'd fit inside her.

"Don't be scared, *reinita*. I'd never hurt you."

Now they were here and he had her all but naked, he couldn't stop himself from taking her. Nothing else mattered. All his doubts were gone from his mind. All he knew was that he needed her on a soul deep level, and maybe, just maybe, her purity would rub off on him rather than the other way around.

"I know you won't mean to…"

Jessie cut her words off by scooping her up in his arms. He loved how her weight felt in his embrace, and how her soft skin felt against his hard muscles. Gently, he lowered her to the mattress and kissed her softly before he rose from her.

"Trust me to make this good for you, *reinita*."

Forcing his body to remain still he waited for her to respond. Mentally pleading with her to say yes, it felt like an age before she nodded her head. A breath he hadn't realized he'd been holding whooshed from his lungs and he leaned in to take a grip on either side of her g-string. She lifted her butt to allow him to pull it from her hips. Unable to resist his need to touch her, he caressed her skin as he slid the scrap of material all the way off her legs. He could feel her body jump and he glanced up to her face to see her chest rising and falling with jerky movements, while her eyes were a little wider than normal. Stroking her calves gently, Jessie took a calming breath as he wracked his brain for a way to ease her fear. Something inside him cracked at seeing her so vulnerable. He bet his strong, stubborn Kit had never in her life, looked as raw and exposed as she did right now.

Holding her gaze, he lifted his hands from her legs and took her foot in his palms. He carefully slid free her stiletto and began to rub the arch of her foot. The ache in his chest eased a fraction as she groaned and relaxed a little. Leaning down, he trailed kisses from her ankle up the smooth skin of her calf. When he reached the tender skin behind her knee, he gave it a little nip, and she gasped, then giggled.

"Damn, that tickles."

He took an easy breath. She was where he wanted her to be now. Relaxed and enjoying his touch. With a chuckle, he stroked her leg as he returned to the mattress and repeated the process on the other side. But this time he didn't stop at her knee. He kept going to where he was dying to be. He kissed up her thigh until he got near the neatly trimmed red curls covering her mound. The smell of her arousal filled his mind and he inhaled deeply as he ran the tip of his nose up the crease between her thigh and torso. He wanted to bathe in her scent, absorb it so far inside himself that he'd never take another breath without being reminded of her. He laid a kiss over her hipbone as he gazed up to her face. Pride filled his body, strengthening him as he took in the splashes of color over her cheeks, her clear eyes and heated gaze. Her lips were parted while she watched him. He alone did that to her.

With a smile, he lowered to press his lips against her soft, tender skin as he worked his way over to where he was dying to be. Using his palms, he spread her thighs a little wider as he covered her core with his mouth. With a gasp, Kit arched beneath him, and Jessie held her hips down so he could use the flat of his tongue to swipe from back to front. He tightened his grip as she thrashed against his hold as he went back for more, purring at the taste of her cream as it filled his mouth and slid down his throat. *So that's what heaven tastes like.*

"What are you doing to me?"

Her hoarse whisper sent shivers down his spine and he lifted away from her a fraction, "I'm taking care of you, *reinita.*"

He blew a stream of air over her slick flesh, and she shuddered as she became even wetter. Still purring, he lowered to lap at her. His desire for her became all-consuming; he was like a dying man in a desert who just found a fresh water spring.

And he intended to drink until he was full.

A whimper left her as her spine bowed off the mattress and she gripped her fingers into his hair. She alternated between holding him close and pulling him away from her core, like she couldn't make up her mind if she wanted more or for the pleasure to stop. She was on the edge of climaxing, and he wondered if this would be her first. He moved to suckle her clit into his mouth as he slid one, then two fingers into her tight channel. He moaned as he thought of how she was going to feel gripping his erection, all slick, soft and snug against his hard flesh.

Her thighs tensed and she cried out as she released her hold on him to slap the mattress. Her internal walls clenched around his fingers, and he wanted to see her expression as she came for him. He glanced up her body. Kit had her head thrown back and her mouth open as she panted. Her fists were tightly balled in the sheets as her body quivered and squirmed in his grip. His breath caught at how wild and beautiful she looked in the throes of an orgasm. He would *never* forget the sight of her as she was now. His own body reacted to hers, his now painfully hard erection throbbing as if to remind him it was still waiting for its turn.

With a small groan, he moved up her body, kissing his way to her mouth. He pulled up short and his heart stuttered when he saw the tear tracks down her cheeks.

"Kit, *reinita*. I didn't hurt you, did I?"

Jessie frowned as he tried to think of how he might have caused her pain. He understood the first time a woman had sex it could hurt, but he didn't think him stretching her a little with his fingers would have caused her enough discomfort to make her cry.

"Not hurt. Just a little overwhelmed."

Jessie smiled down at Kit as his heart resumed beating

normally. He felt a prickle behind his eyes at how sweet she was. All her toughness had melted away and she was totally bare to him now. He could see the vulnerability in her gaze as she looked up at him from where she still twitched beneath him.

With his instincts screaming at him to take her and make her his, he reached for the condom and moved to kneel between her thighs. As he rolled the latex down his shaft, he couldn't drag his gaze from where she bit her lower lip as she watched him. Once he was finished, he covered her body with his and kissed her long and deep. She'd tensed up a little and he wanted her totally relaxed when he entered her. Kit wrapped her arms around his neck and ran her fingers up into his hair as he devoured her mouth. While she was focused on his lips, he trailed his palm down her body until he could grip his erection and line himself up with her slick entrance. He held his breath as he entered her and was enveloped in pure ecstasy. She stilled beneath him, and he pulled out a fraction before he began to rock himself in and out of her channel. She gasped and squirmed, then made the sexiest damn noises he'd ever heard as he slowly buried more of his length inside her. He'd been right; she was snug against his hard flesh. He could barely think straight. There was no way he could last long this first time, not with all her heat surrounding him and her having put her trust in him to take care of her.

Using every ounce of patience he had, he worked his way inside her with small thrusts. All the while he kissed her lips and face, before he nibbled his way up to her ear. Kit ran her hands over his back and shoulders as she moved with him, until he fully seated himself. With a pained gasp, she stiffened and clung to him. He held himself completely motionless, allowing her time to adjust to him. His lungs began to burn as breaths rasped in and out, and he felt sweat bead and drip from his body. Everything inside him demanded he take her, to thrust into her until he reached completion and claimed her. But his need to care for her allowed him to hold off from pounding into her like a wild animal in heat.

When Jessie thrust deep inside her, a sharp jolt of pain stole her breath. Kit held him tightly against her as she panted through it. She'd known, in theory, losing her virginity would hurt, but she'd not realized how a flare of pain in the midst of intense pleasure would feel. As it began to dissipate, she slid her fingers from where she gripped his shoulders up into his hair. She allowed the soft, silky feel of it against her skin to distract her from the mixed sensations swirling between her thighs. He nibbled at her jaw, laying tender kisses over her face. In response to his ministrations, her muscles began to loosen and relax. Desire rose up over everything else as the ache subsided and she arched beneath him. Jessie groaned and his erection twitched inside of her, causing her to tighten her grip in his hair as arousal spiraled through her body. Planting the soles of her feet flat on the bed, she hesitantly tilted her hips, and the feel of him sliding into her a little deeper felt divine. She purred when he shuddered as he started thrusting slowly into her. Instinctively, she moved her pelvis in time with his strokes. He was a huge presence inside of her and she loved the feel of his hot length gliding in and out of her core. There was no pain now, only pleasure. Sweet hot ribbons of desire wound through her body as Jessie made love to her.

She looked up at his face and her heart picked up speed. His eyes were closed and a small frown creased his brow in concentration. The muscles of his neck stood out and his arms on either side of her were tense and shiny with sweat. She whispered his name and she heard the ache in her voice. His silver blue irises opened and with a low growl, he took her mouth in a rough kiss. A shudder ran through her at the feel of his stubble against her skin. It was little rough but felt so damn good she didn't care that he was no doubt leaving marks on her.

"I need more of you, *reinita*."

She frowned at Jessie's comment. They were naked and intimately joined together — how exactly did he expect to get 'more'? A gasp left her throat as he quickly and smoothly slid free of her body and flipped her onto her front. Within moments he had her on her hands and knees on the edge of the mattress as he stood behind her. Kit moaned at the empty feeling inside her core while her mind whirled with arousal at how easily Jessie had manhandled her into position. She was around six feet and muscular, and no one had ever treated her like Jessie did. He made her feel feminine, like he wanted to not just make love to her but possess her body and soul.

Kit screamed out as Jessie slid back into her overly sensitive tissues with one long thrust of his thick erection. With a firm grip on her hips, he took her hard. Her skin slicked with sweat as she panted and pushed back against him while he pounded into her. She clenched her fists into the bedding as her body began to tighten. His left hand snaked up from her hip to rest between her breasts where he pushed up. She shook with the ease he lifted her weight from the bed.

When her back pressed against his chest, she reached her hands over to run her fingers into Jessie's hair which was now damp with his perspiration.

"Feels. So. Good. Kit."

He punctuated each word with another thrust into her, pushing her even higher.

"You're not so bad yourself."

She was surprised at how husky her voice was. When he pulled at her nipple with his left hand, she hissed out her breath. It caused a ribbon of heat to spiral down to her lower belly, and his right hand seemed to follow its path as he moved to press against her clit with his clever fingers. Panting, she tried to hold off her climax. She wasn't ready for this to be over. She wanted to stay connected with Jessie, stay like this for the rest of her life, or at the very least, for the entirety of the night. His thrusts turned jerky as his breathing went choppy.

Unable to hold off any longer, she threw her head

back against Jessie's shoulder with a scream as she came hard. Jessie's hands tightened on her breast and hip while he buried his face against her neck and went still. He growled when she felt him twitch inside of her as he came. Kit smiled and let her eyes close as a glow began to spread over her.

With a jerk and a curse, Jessie tore himself free of her, shattering her contentment. Still a little lost in her post-climatic haze, she took a nosedive onto the mattress. What the hell? With her defensive instincts flaring, she turned on Jessie with a growl.

"What the fuck, Jessie?"

His face was ghost white and he staggered away until his back pressed against the wall. His whole body trembled enough she could see it in the dim lighting as he held his right wrist with his left hand and stared at the claws coming out of his otherwise human fingers.

"Why the hell do I have claws? I've *never* partly shifted before."

Kit rubbed her face with her palms, trying not to feel deserted by his panic. Of course he wouldn't know about the mating ritual. *Dammit!* She'd been too tipsy to think of that before. Of course, the moment Jessie stripped her bare, any residual alcohol in her system vanished, burned away with the heat of their passion. Which meant as she sat here shivering as though she'd been doused in ice water, she had to deal with Jessie's rejection of her while stone sober.

With a deep breath, she forced her voice to remain

level. Kit would not allow him to hear how much he'd hurt her.

"You have claws so you can mark me. It's part of the mating ritual. Guess Jake hasn't explained that to you yet?"

Feeling vulnerable and exposed, she tugged the sheet from the bed and wrapped it around herself as she sat with her knees pulled up against the ache in her chest.

"When shifter mates make love, and climax together, the male will sprout claws on his right hand. Traditionally, he then scrapes his claws over her right hip. It doesn't cut into her skin, but with magic leaves behind a set of four scratch marks revealing snow leopard spots beneath. Once the female is marked, her right hand sprouts claws. She then leaves a similar mark over the male's heart on his left pectoral. The marks are a sign to the rest of the world that they are bound and unavailable. It's sacred and very special."

She ground her teeth as she blinked rapidly to stop the tears pricking her eyes from falling. Everything about tonight had been so sublime. She'd loved every moment but now watching Jessie's face drain of even more color as he shook his head, she felt hollow inside. Bile rose in her throat as dread filled her. They'd not discussed what Jessie's plans for tomorrow were at all. Was he planning on leaving? Had he not intended to sleep with her tonight, before they'd had a little too much to drink and got carried away?

Lowering her face, she wiped her wet eyes against her

knees. With her heart in her throat, she looked back to Jessie in time to see his claws disappear and his fingernails reappear in their place. With her cheek resting on her knees, she did nothing to stop the fresh wave of tears as through blurry eyes she watched Jessie rush to dress. Clearly on the verge of panic, he silently ran for the door, shattering her soul and breaking her heart as he glanced back for a moment with a haunted look in his eyes before slipping out her door.

Standing in the departure lounge at Hobart Airport, Jessie rubbed the back of his stiff neck. He had to visit his mama on the anniversary of her passing. Damn, he wished she was alive to help him work out what to do. Bloody hell, he'd known sleeping with Kit would end badly. Of course, he didn't think it would be because he'd panic after nearly mating her by accident, then run out on her. He squeezed his eyes shut against the image that was now burned into his brain.

After he'd dressed and had the door in his hand, he hadn't been able to resist the urge to look back to the bed. Kit had been sitting there wrapped in a white sheet with her cheek resting on her knees as she watched him. The light had reflected off the tears leaving her reddened eyes. Fuck, he wanted to kick his own ass for making her cry. Kit wasn't the kind of woman who'd cry at just anything. He'd hurt her, and like a coward he'd run from her room back to his. He'd woken Pedro as he slammed his way into the room and his friend gave him a disapproving look while shaking his head before he rolled over and went back to sleep, leaving Jessie to deal with his inner turmoil alone.

For as long as he lived, he knew he'd never forget the image she'd made. She'd looked fragile, broken and so damn innocent. He was a bastard to have reduced such a strong woman to tears like he had. He rubbed his chest as he blindly looked out the window. The ache in his heart would not go away. The overhead speaker announced his flight was boarding and he picked up his backpack and followed Pedro to the check-in line. Pedro hadn't said a word all morning. Instinct told him Pedro had worked out that he'd messed up with Kit. Of course, Pedro had no way of knowing exactly how, but still, his friend knew.

By the time he settled in his seat next to Pedro at Melbourne Airport ready to take off to Santiago, Chile, he'd had all he could take of the silence.

"You haven't said a word to me all morning. Something up?"

After Pedro took way more care fastening his seat belt than it required, he turned to look Jessie in the eye before he spoke in their native Spanish.

"When you stormed back into our room last night, I figured you'd done something stupid. I assumed by morning you'd wake up to yourself and go to Kit to sort it out. But no. You kept running like a scared little boy. You didn't see her in the lobby as we left did you?"

Releasing a heavy breath, Jessie's shoulders slumped down. He'd felt her presence but he hadn't been brave enough to look over to her. He couldn't stand to see the pain he'd caused her written all over her beautiful features.

"I knew she was there. But no, I didn't actually see her."

"Kit is a good woman. She's tough, more than strong enough to handle you and all your crap, but you didn't even give her a chance did you? The woman I saw this morning was not the same one who sat with us last night. This morning she wasn't happy or joking, she was holding on to a false front by the tips of her fingers from the look of it. At a glance, she appeared the same as normal, but I saw how her skin had paled since yesterday, how her eyes are now rimmed in red. When she handed over her room key to the receptionist, her fingers were trembling. How could you do that to her? I don't know what you did last night between leaving the gala and returning to our room but whatever it was, it wasn't right." He paused to sigh and take a deep breath. "I'm quiet because I want to rip you apart you for hurting her. I'm not one of you. I don't pretend to understand all that being one of your kind entails, but I've got eyes, man. I saw what was happening between the two of you and it was good. When you weren't being an idiot, you two looked right together, happy. Now you're both miserable, and I'm thinking that's solely on you. So, we have about fourteen hours ahead of us with not much to fill the time. I strongly suggest you have a good look at yourself, buddy. Have a long think about what your future's going to be like. You want a family some day? Kit's your shot at that. And don't start in on the 'what if I'm like my father' crap. Kit would put you on your ass in a heartbeat if you even attempted to lay a hand on her, not that you would, because you're more your mama's boy than your father's. In your whole life, you've never laid a hand on a woman or a child. Why the hell do you think you'd start now?"

Jessie opened his mouth to respond, but Pedro shut him down with a sharp shake of his head before he plugged in his headphones and turned away from him. *Fuck.* He couldn't lose Pedro's friendship. With a heavy heart, Jessie leaned back into his chair and stared at the small screen in front of him as it showed the safety procedures he knew by heart after having flown so often. He glanced at Pedro and could tell by the firm set of his jaw he was clenching it. With a sigh, he pulled out his own headphones and plugged them in before he scrolled through the radio options and cranked up a classic rock station.

With a deep breath, he closed his eyes and absorbed the pain that over took his heart and head. Not being near Kit was a physical ache, which worsened the further away from her he got. Knowing he was the one who forced the separation was like adding razor blades to the pain slicing into his soul.

As the plane left Australian soil and took to the sky, he wondered what the fuck he was doing. Pedro was right. *Of course.* He should never have left Tasmania, especially without at least talking to Kit. He ran his thumb over the tips of his fingers on his right hand as he remembered how his claws had appeared as he'd climaxed inside of her. Damn, he hoped he hadn't totally ruined both their lives by not mating her. Would he get another chance? Or was the mating ritual a one-time thing that once it happened that was it? He felt the sting of tears but with a quiet growl, refused to allow them to fall.

The next fourteen hours were going to be some of the longest of his life.

Jake sat behind a desk that used to be his with a sense of déjà vu. He didn't regret his decision to hand over the Captaincy to Dominic, but he'd be lying if he said he didn't miss it. With half the crew off helping pack up the Rally, they were down to a skeleton staff. Not that Jake minded with all the crap going on with Conner and Tina. In fact, he rather liked the distraction. His mobile went off and seeing it was Nick, one of the shifters on the rally crew, he answered it quickly.

"Hey, Nick, how's the pack up going?"

"Hi, Jake. Pack up's going fine. But Kit is not."

Jake sat forward in his seat as his mind whirled with concern.

"What happened? I heard she left the gala with Jessie last night, I'd hoped they'd sorted out their differences."

"Kit isn't talking, Jake. At all, to anyone. I can confirm she left with him last night. They looked tight when I saw them walking out of the gala. But today, she's not herself. She's trying to be. But it's a front. And I just got word that Jessie flew out this morning back to Chile."

"Bloody hell, that boy is a moron. Thanks for the heads up. I'll send Sophie over. Just keep an eye on her until then, okay? I don't want anyone pushing and for her to lash out."

"Sure can. We've made sure she's not been alone since that idiot attacked her the other day. We'll always take care of our leap sister. You know that. It's how you taught us to be."

Jake couldn't help but smile. Being alpha was damn hard, but it was nice when you got a little affirmation that you'd done at least some of it right.

"Thanks, Nick. You're a good man. I'll see you at the debriefing, if not before."

After hanging up, he quickly dialed his wife to ask her to go find Kit. Once he mentioned Jessie had left for Chile this morning, his sweet mate couldn't get moving fast enough to go to their leap daughter. Poor Kit must be hurting so much with Jessie abandoning her. Jake hoped she'd be able to find a way to move forward. He couldn't imagine what it would feel like to be rejected by your destined mate.

Glancing at the clock, he quickly worked out it was late evening in Chile. He needed to ring Fernando. Honestly, he should have already rung the alpha of the South American Continental leap about Jessie but with everything going on with Conner and Tina, and now with

Trigger in the area, he'd not had the time. Conveniently, Fernando Molina lived in Arica, the same city Jessie called home. Jake hoped Fernando could talk some sense into the stupid boy.

Picking up the landline on the desk, he dialed his fellow alpha.

"*Hola*, Jake. It's not like you to call so late. What's happened?"

"Hi, Fernando, sorry for the lateness of the call. Have you got a few minutes to chat?"

"Sure, I was just settling in for the night. Got all the time in the world."

"We've found the other South American comet shifter."

"Well, that's wonderful news, especially if he's found his way to you and your leap daughter. Is it not going well?"

"His name is Jessie Lutrec."

"The rally driver? Who lives in the very city I've lived in my whole life?"

"The one and the same. He came to Tassie for a rally and ran into Kit, who was volunteering at the event. Jessie hadn't ever met another shifter before, Fernando. I've spoken with him a couple of times but due to a crazy woman trying to murder my youngest son's mate, I've not had all that much free time."

"Gee, Jake. Since when was Tasmania crime central for Australia?"

"I have no idea, but it would appear it's going to get

worse before it gets better. We now have Trigger here coming after our leap. They've attacked Kit, attempting to take her."

"Damn. So what did Jessie do about that?"

"He turned up just as Kit dealt with the situation. That female's been very well trained. It would take a bloody ninja to get the jump on her. I believe Jessie is struggling with a few things. He's obviously in a little shock that he's not the only shifter out in the world, but he's also unsure of his place with Kit. He can feel the attraction and connection but he can also see she's more than capable of taking care of herself. I also sense something really horrible went down after his first shift. He hasn't confided in me what, but there's definitely something there."

"Jake, if Jessie is there in Tassie, why are you telling me all this?"

"Because the stupid fool flew out this morning to go home. I've only just been told so I'm not sure what happened. All I know is they left a gala dinner together last night and this morning Kit's an empty shell of herself and Jessie's gone."

Fernando let loose a string of Spanish that didn't sound happy, "The young and foolish will always be the bane of an alpha's life."

"Couldn't agree with you more, my friend."

Jake gave Fernando Jessie's phone number and other details before he hung up. Then he sat back in the chair and rubbed his eyes on a sigh.

"I gather from that conversation we're going to have watch Kit."

Jake glanced up at his eldest son. Dominic was going to be the next alpha, so in the past few months Jake had been letting him in on information the rest of the leap weren't privy to.

"I think so. Something happened last night, then this morning he flew out. I don't know how Kit will recover from the blow, but I doubt it's going to be pleasant."

He loved Kit as a daughter, but he was certain she'd only allowed him to see a fraction of her skills. He knew how dangerous she could be if she lost her mind and went wild. Add in Trigger chasing her tail and this situation had the makings for a bloody bad ending.

Before he could think any more about it, his phone rang once more. Not recognizing the number, he answered with caution.

"Hello, Jake White here."

"Hi, Jake, it's Detective Alex Ross. Have you got a moment or two?"

Jake was ninety-nine percent sure he wasn't going to like what the good detective was about to say, but Jake had helped him out a time or two when they got truly stuck on a case and couldn't refuse the man. Alex knew about the shifters and also knew sometimes animal instincts could pick up on things humans couldn't.

"Sure, Alex. What can I help you with?"

Chapter Seven

Her leap brothers were driving her nuts. Kit knew they'd heard about Jessie leaving, just like they knew she'd left the gala with him last night. She appreciated that they cared about her, but they were just about smothering her. She couldn't turn around without running into one of them. Jessie's rejection had cut her to her core. She'd struggled to drag herself from bed this morning. She'd not slept well and her insides felt like they'd taken a beating.

Even now, hours later, her chest still ached and her stomach continued to constantly churn. She hadn't been able to eat all day, which didn't help her deal with anything. In an attempt to simply get through her day in one piece, she was trying to focus on work. Cleaning and packing up after the rally took ages. Kit was currently with Nick collecting road closure signs from one of the roadblocks, so for a while she only had one leap brother to deal with, although, he was starting to seriously get on her nerves.

"I can lift a damn sign on my own, Nick."

"Yeah, I know, Kit. I'm just trying to help."

The sound of an approaching vehicle had Kit glancing

up the road. A light blue Suzuki Swift pulled up, and she growled low as she spun on Nick.

"You called Jake in on me?"

He shrugged before resting his fists against his hips. "Only because we're all worried about you, Kit. I didn't do it to cause trouble, just figured you'd need someone to talk to and Sophie would be a better choice than any of us men."

The expression of pity and concern on Nick's face was enough to make her want to hit something. She didn't need coddling, dammit!

"I don't want to talk about it at all, Nick. How would you feel if your mate slept with you, then ran off like a fucking scared little rabbit to the other side of the world?"

"It'd hurt like a bitch, Kit. It would feel like my heart had been torn out. So, go with Sophie and let her help you deal with it."

Nick's features had hardened as he spoke, and Kit knew she wasn't going to get anywhere by arguing with him. Fury flared bright inside her and she wanted to lash out, to make something else hurt instead of her, even if it only lasted for a moment. Knowing she'd regret flattening Nick, she hefted the sign and all but threw it into the rear of the Council Ute they were using. The sound of metal grinding against metal made her wince, and she hoped she didn't just wreck the damn sign. With no humans around, she'd not cared about restraining her supernatural strength.

She glanced around the ground near her to find anything else she could vent on. She was still tempted to throw down with Nick but even as her mind was clouded in a haze of rage, she knew he'd only acted out of concern for her. She didn't want to ever hurt any of her leap family, and she knew she'd have done the same for him if the roles were reversed. A quiet whine caught her attention and she turned to see Kelly's dalmatian, Raksha, sitting a little way away from her, looking up at her with sad eyes. Damn dog saw deeper into her than he should. She wriggled her fingers toward him.

"C'mere, boy."

He rushed over to nuzzle into her palm, and she dropped down to give the animal a cuddle. Kit had never liked dogs. Even before she knew she was part feline she'd not liked canines at all. But this little guy who'd been the sole survivor of a madman's rage against his mother and litter-mates, had pulled her heart strings from the get go. The same madman had put young Kelly in the hospital for a while too so Kit had babysat the dog when he was just a puppy. Since then, Raksha seemed to always know when she was feeling out of sorts. He'd turn up at her place out of the blue some days, having run off on Dominic, Adele or Kelly while they walked him.

Releasing the pup and feeling a little calmer, she turned back to see if Kelly was with Sophie. Relief flooded Kit when she saw it was only Sophie who stood waiting for her. Of course, being the middle of the day, Kelly must be in school. Raksha didn't like being left alone so he either hung out at the fire station or with Sophie.

"So you brought Raksha to help you take me away?"

"We just want to help, Kit. But I think it wise if you leave clean-up for the others. Especially while we're unsure if Trigger are targeting you."

Shit. She'd forgotten about the idiot who had tried to grab her.

"Yeah, okay. I'm going. Nick, you shouldn't be out here on your own either."

"I'll be all right. I'm going to finish up here then I'll go back and grab one of the guys to help with the rest."

"I'll help you finish up before we go."

Kit spun around to ask Sophie if she minded waiting when her vision fogged and she stumbled. *Shit.* Physical labor out in the summer sun with an empty stomach never ended well. She should know better.

"Whoa, Kit." Nick's strong grip wrapped around her biceps and led her over to Sophie's Swift. Kit's head was a mess and being out in the hot summer sun was the last place she wanted to be, but she didn't want to leave Nick alone now that she remembered there were potentially men after them.

"Go, Kit. You're the only one they've singled out so far. I'll be fine."

"When was the last time you ate, Kit?"

She felt her cheeks heat under Sophie's scrutiny.

"I, ah, I'm not sure."

Sophie sighed. "C'mon, Kit, let's go to our place. I'll

fix you something and we can relax for a bit."

With a sigh, Kit allowed Nick to open her door for her so she could sit in the cool interior of the vehicle. The bright sunlight was hurting her eyes and she felt light headed. She rubbed the bridge of her nose after clicking her seat belt. Her rage had drained from her and she was left feeling empty and so damn tired. She didn't have the energy to argue with either Nick or Sophie, and knew her dizzy spell had sealed the deal. She squinted out the windscreen to see Sophie speaking to Nick before she brought Raksha over and put the pup into the back seat. Kit watched Nick with concern as Sophie settled into the driver's side.

"Not sure we should be leaving Nick alone, Soph."

"He promised to be careful and keep an eye out for anything suspicious. He's also going to call me when he gets back to base."

Kit still had a sour feeling in her gut but she'd been feeling off all morning. She hated that all her instincts were out of kilter. She'd always relied on them to keep her safe in the past.

"So, Kit. Want to tell me what happened with Jessie?"

"Not really, Soph."

"Well, if you change your mind, you know where to find me."

"Yeah, I know. Maybe one day but not now. Not while it's still so raw. I just can't."

"Fair enough, kitten."

Sophie left her in peace as they drove back to

Rosebery. Kit closed her eyes and tilted her face toward the window, allowing the sun's heat to warm her skin. An image of Jessie rushing out the door of her hotel room filled her vision a moment later and a cold chill rose up her spine, taking away any heat she'd gained from the sunshine. From the moment he'd pulled away from her after their lovemaking, she'd felt a kernel of ice form in her center. As the hours of the night ticked by, the chill increased until now she felt it in her fingertips and toes. Would she ever feel warm again?

When Sophie turned the engine off, Kit blinked her eyes open to see they'd pulled up at Jake and Sophie's place. On autopilot, she slipped from the vehicle and set Raksha free from the back seat. She turned toward the house and followed Sophie inside. As they entered the foyer, Sophie pulled her phone free with a frown.

"Nick should have called in by now."

The sour feeling in her gut turned rancid. Something was wrong. She just knew it. It hadn't been the situation with Jessie that had her stomach in knots on the drive back. Kit watched Sophie as she attempted to call him.

"No answer."

"We have to go back and look for him."

"I know, Kit. I just wish Jake wasn't working at the station today."

"Give me the keys, Sophie. I'll drive while you ring around."

Sophie glared at her. "I don't think so. You run into the kitchen and grab something out of the fridge to eat before you pass out on me. I'll ring around while you do. Then we'll head back and pick up the boys from the rally and go look."

All thoughts of Jessie vanished as Kit's heart was in her throat with fear for her leap brother's safety as she bolted toward the kitchen. She knew better than to argue with Sophie about it, and she was still light headed. She needed some food to keep her going until they found Nick. Kit prayed they made it to him in time.

With great care Jessie brushed away the dried leaves from his mama's headstone. Tears burned his eyes as he arranged the roses into the vase embedded into the top edge of the marble. Two years later and the pain of losing his precious mother was still raw enough to bring him to his knees.

For so long it had been just the two of them. Tatiana Lutrec had not been simply a strong woman, she'd been kind and compassionate too. She never once rejected or judged him for being different. When he'd shifted to leopard form around her, she'd rough up his fur and lay her cheek against his head. Damn, he missed her so much. With the gravel biting into his shins through the material of his pants, he stayed kneeling before her grave. He lowered his face as his tears flowed.

His emotions were a mess. The grief for his mother was dominating at the moment, but Kit's absence was a permanent hole in his soul as well. He'd barely been able to function since he flew home. Kit was always on his mind, and last night as he'd tried to settle in to sleep, pain wracked his heart like he'd been stabbed. Jessie had lain awake all damn night. He knew Kit was in agony and he was too far away to reach her. She refused his calls and his attempts to dream bond with her. Although, that was tricky with the time difference. Maybe he should try giving Jake a call...

With a sigh, he looked up at the words engraved on the marble. This would be the last time he'd come for who knew how long. Before the plane had landed, he'd made the decision to pack up and move to Australia. He had to be close to Kit. Every cell of his body craved her and he was completely miserable without her.

Pedro was still giving him the cold shoulder, although Jessie knew he'd snap out of it as soon as he learned Jessie intended to return to Kit and grovel until she forgave him.

"Goodbyes are never easy are they, brother?"

He rubbed his face with his hand quickly to wipe away the remaining tears as he jerked around at the deep voice he didn't know. He took a deep inhale and sensed this man was like him. A shifter. But he had no clue who he was.

"No, they're not. Do I know you?"

The older man smiled with warmth. "I am Fernando Molina and I am the alpha of the leap here in Chile. Jake called me and told me where I might find you. He also mentioned you probably had some questions about what you learned on your trip to Australia. If you've finished here, would you care to join me for a coffee?"

Jessie took in the other man, trying to work out if he should trust him. He looked honest enough and he could imagine Jake calling in someone to help him after he learned Jessie had left.

"Yeah, I was just about to leave so I can come with you."

"Excellent. I know a place not too far from here where we'll be left in peace to speak."

Twenty minutes later, Jessie found himself sitting in a small cafe at a table out on a balcony. The tables around them were all empty so they would be able to speak relatively freely.

"I'm much like Jake, Jessie. I'm here for you and you can tell me anything you like. Everything you say to me is held in confidence and I promise to pass no judgment on you or reject anything about you."

Jessie released a huff; he was pretty sure if he told Fernando he'd murdered his father that 'no judgment' thing would be blown out of the water pretty damn quick. What could he start with that would test if the man really was as trustworthy as he claimed?

"Can you tell me why I was in agony last night when there was nothing physically wrong with me?"

For a moment Fernando clenched his jaw, and Jessie noticed his left eye twitch before the man zoned his gaze in on Jessie's once again.

"Part of the mating is that you'll feel each other's emotions. But only the extreme ones. Things like jamming your finger in a door or getting angry over losing your car keys aren't enough. As to why you felt it last night, that's another story." He took a drink of his coffee before he continued. Jessie knew something big must have happened and the fact it had to involve Kit had his instincts flaring. Not that he could do anything. Stupid bastard that he was, he had run away to the other side of the world on her.

"Jake called an urgent meeting of the Council of Alphas late last night, which would have been early afternoon for them. A member of Jake's leap, Nicolas Larson, was attacked yesterday. He and Kit were packing up roadblocks when Jake got word of you having run off. Worried for Kit, he sent Sophie to go collect her. Silly girl hadn't eaten all day and nearly passed out so Sophie took her. Nick told the ladies he'd finish up the block they were working on then go collect more help. When he didn't call in to let them know he was okay as they'd agreed, Sophie and Kit grabbed a couple of the boys and went looking. They found the vehicle he was using, along with a large amount of blood. No body, but Trigger does that. They like to keep their kills. Bastards."

Jessie's body went numb. This was his fault? Or had his leaving saved Kit from the same fate as Nick?

"Jake couldn't tell me much about Trigger. Can you shed some light on who the hell they are?"

Jessie didn't think the small amount he'd learned from the internet was worth mentioning.

"Well, that's a loaded question. Publicly, Trigger

Corporation is a research company. They mainly deal with pharmaceuticals. Trigger Corporation has denied numerous times that they are linked with the Trigger gangs that have attacked shifter communities over the years. In my opinion, the fact both their logos consist of the same picture rather gives them away. Unfortunately, they leave very little behind when they attack and they always take the bodies, both theirs and ours. With no evidence aside from missing people, the police can't do much."

"And you're telling me there's a Trigger gang in Tasmania right now?"

"Yes, I am. I'm also telling you that Jake believes they are targeting Kit. Nick was a strong shifter, in his prime. He would not have gone down easily. If Trigger were looking for easy targets, they would have gone for either the older or the younger leap members. There are certainly easier targets, shifters whose lives are predictable. Honestly, the only way they could have known, not only where Nick was, but also that he was alone, was if they'd been following him and Kit. Jake mentioned an attempt on Kit previously. We believe that she is the target. What we can't work out yet is why."

Jessie thought back to the man who had attempted to take Kit. She was strong, but she wasn't immortal. If her attacker hadn't been alone, if there'd been more of them, Kit would have been killed or taken. The very thought of Kit being harmed in any way made his blood run cold as every protective instinct he possessed rose up.

"So get Jake to force Kit on a plane over here. I'll take care of her."

Fernando cocked a brow at him. "I was under the impression you had rejected the bond between yourself and Kit. Why would Jake send her to you?"

The growl snuck out before Jessie could stop it. "Because she's my mate. And I'm a fool. I'd already decided that I would return to Australia to be with Kit. But if it's not safe for her there, then she should come here."

A wide grin broke over Fernando's face. "Well, I'm glad to hear you've seen the light in regards to your mate, Jessie. But Jake still can't force her onto a plane. For one, I strongly doubt a woman like Kit would ever abandon her leap family. But the main reason is Trigger have proved that while they appear to be targeting Kit, they will take out any shifter they manage to get alone. Jake wouldn't dare ask her to leave at this point."

Jessie thought it through. Fernando was right of course.

"And the bastards could follow her here and bring your leap to their attention too."

"It's 'our' leap, son. And while true, not our main concern. If bringing Kit here was the best way to keep her safe, I wouldn't hesitate."

Jessie forced the lump down from where it clogged his throat at Fernando's easy acceptance of him into the leap.

"I was going to take a few days to get everything

sorted before I left to go back, but now I can't wait. My instincts are screaming at me to keep her protected."

"I bet they are. Write a list of all the things that need doing. I'll take care of it for you, Jessie."

With a trembling hand, Jessie rubbed his jaw. He couldn't quite believe he suddenly had all these people—shifters—willing to help him.

"Thank you, Fernando. I guess I better get moving and see when I can get a flight."

He hoped Kit wouldn't simply kick his ass to the curb when he arrived on her doorstep.

Jake stared across his kitchen table at their latest houseguest. Jessie had been living here since he returned from Chile last week. Jake guessed the boy had hoped Kit would just welcome him back with open arms and he'd move in with her straight away. Just proved Jessie didn't know Kit too well. That girl could hold a grudge and did not handle rejection well.

"So, Jessie, what're your plans for this evening?"

"Same as always, Jake. I'll guard Kit and make sure nothing happens to her. You never know, today might be my lucky day and she'll actually speak to me."

Jake chuckled at Jessie's fatalistic speech. "She will eventually, and don't feel too badly. Kit hasn't really spoken to anyone since Nick was killed."

His chest ached at the loss. Sophie had told him how neither her nor Kit had wanted to leave him alone. Typical of a young unmated male shifter, Nick had refused their advice to immediately come back to base to get someone to help him. Now he was gone.

"Just make sure you're never alone either, Jessie."

"None of us are, Jake. The teams took your advice seriously."

With a nod, Jake picked up his coffee cup and took a swig. Between the attack on Nick and the sudden increase in petty crimes, the police couldn't catch a break. Jake had asked for volunteers to form two teams to investigate and guard the town. Naturally, Kit insisted on being involved. She was the only female on the teams but the whole leap knew better than to try to stop her from being out there. Taking shifts, Rosebery had shifter guards roaming the streets for about twenty hours a day.

"Did Choden know anything?"

Having Choden in town briefly for the memorial for Kelly's mother, Jake had mentioned to Jessie he would ask him about Trigger.

"Unfortunately not. Choden's exact abilities are a mystery to all of us. I have no idea how they work, but I do know he can't call on them for a specific situation."

"Does Choden know when Trigger first came into being?"

Jake shook his head. "Not specifically, it was the early 1900s when Choden started hearing reports of entire leaps being wiped out. He assumes that was the early incarnation of Trigger."

"Has to be frustrating to have all those powers but not be able to call on them when he needs them."

Jake fully agreed with Jessie on that one. "Yes, it's highly aggravating. Choden cares deeply for every snow leopard shifter and it cuts him deeply every time one of us is hurt. Actually, speaking of Trigger, I need to call another meeting of the teams. Alex rang me earlier with some information I need to pass on."

He wasn't sure telling Alex about Trigger's hatred of shifters was a good move, but now it looked like it was the right thing to do. Alex was willing to believe Jake and said he'd quietly check into the company. Jake had warned him not to do anything obvious. Jake was fairly certain Trigger had people on the force. How else had they managed to escape prosecution for so long?

"Do you think we can meet today? Maybe this afternoon when we change shift?"

Jessie's question pulled Jake from his thoughts.

"Ah, yeah, that would be best. Might head up to the Cradle Mountain National Park. We can get a run in too. All this stress has everyone on edge."

Jake rose from the table to go to his office. "I'll make the calls now and get it organized."

It didn't take long to ring around and get everyone to agree to the meeting. He also gave Alex a call to let him know the town was going to be without its paranormal guards for an hour or so tonight. Then he headed back to the kitchen to grab Jessie.

"Okay, we're on but we need to get moving to get there in time."

The drive wasn't too long and Jake pulled into the car

park just as Kit roared in on her bike. Jessie quickly got out and headed toward Kit. Jake looked up in time to catch Kit snarl at him. The female actually curled her lip. Jake had never seen her this hostile before. He rushed from his SUV to talk with the pair. As soon as he was out of the vehicle, the strong waves of anger, hurt and sadness flowed over him, tightening his stomach, but he refused to let it win. This crap couldn't continue, especially while they had Trigger after their tails.

"Enough, Kit. What the hell has gotten into you?"

She moved her glare from Jessie to him. Jake didn't enjoy being roasted by her fury but something had to be done. Jake had told Kit an earlier time, for precisely this purpose. She and Jessie needed to quit circling each other and sort out their issues. It looked like he was going to have to mediate things if he wanted them to get along anytime soon.

"What's gotten into me? Guess Jessie didn't tell you how he blew our chance to mate. Didn't tell you how he panicked when his claws appeared and literally ran from the room when I explained why it had happened?"

"I know Jessie panicked and made a colossal mistake. He's packed up his life in Chile and moved here to sort it out with you, yet you won't give him the time of day. This isn't like you, Kit. What's really going on?"

"I might not know as much about shifters as you do, Jake. But I do know we only get the one mate. That's done with now. The opportunity passed-"

As realization hit him, Jake cut her off. "Stop right

there, Kit. I'm thinking you don't know enough about the mating ceremony. It's not something that is only offered once. Jessie's claws will appear every time until the mating is completed. Shifters only have one true mate in their lifetime, but they have their entire life to complete the bond."

Kit's shoulders slumped as her eyes slid shut before she spoke.

"You mean I'm not destined to be alone forever now? I still have a chance at a family?"

Jake glanced to Jessie in time to see him roll his shoulders while he clenched and released his fists. The pained expression on his face hit him as hard as his strong emotions. Damn, as a leap they needed to educate their young better. His own stomach was still in knots with the level of emotion pouring from both Jessie and Kit but he continued to force it down. Taking control, Jake stepped forward and gave Kit a gentle hug and whispered in her ear, "It's not over, Kit. It's never over, so long as you both breathe. Don't waste time with this grudge, kitten. Who knows how much time any of us have, especially with Trigger after us."

She rested her head against his shoulder and shook as she wept, breaking his heart for her as she did.

"Kit? *Reinita*?"

Jake reached to take her helmet from her as she stood straight to face Jessie.

"Give me your jacket, Kit. I'll lock your gear up in my car. You and Jessie only have a few minutes before the others will begin to arrive."

Kit allowed Jake to take her helmet and leather jacket
before she dashed away the tears from her eyes. She felt
both relieved and incredibly stupid. She'd never heard of
anyone not completing the mating the first time, so she'd
assumed it was a one-time thing. Like them only having
one mate. She took a deep breath in an attempt to level
herself before she faced Jessie.

The moment she saw him her heart melted. She'd
avoided him since he'd arrived, refusing to even glance
in his direction. Now he stood there looking so adorably
nervous. He was looking down while chewing on his
lower lip. Damn, she wanted to kiss that mouth so much.
His gaze rose to meet hers and he rubbed his palms down
his thighs before shaking out his hands. The way he'd run
out on her still hurt, but she needed to give him a chance
to at least explain. Jake was right. Jessie had moved half
way around the globe to be close to her; that had to mean
something. She needed to start acting like an adult. Kit
cocked her head to the side and smiled a little. Jessie took
it as the invitation it was and marched straight up to her.
Within moments she found herself embraced against his
hard muscles, his strong arms wrapped around her. His
large palm pressed her head against his upper chest, and
she felt him nuzzle into her hair and inhale. With her
nose against his collarbone, she was surrounded with his
scent and she felt her body relax against him as she slid
her hands up his back. For the last week she'd kept

herself so tightly coiled she was on the edge of snapping and lashing out. But now, wrapped up with Jessie, she felt the tension ease away and she took a deep breath.

"I'm so sorry, Kit. I thought I'd blown our only chance too. I was hoping you'd still have me without being mated. I can't live without you in my life. By the time the plane landed in Chile I knew I was coming back. Pedro made sure I knew exactly how much of a bastard I was to you. I'm sorry I left without explaining anything. My head was a mess so I stupidly ran. I had to go home to visit my mother's grave. It was the two year anniversary of her passing. But what hurt more than my grief for her was being apart from you. I was already working toward settling everything so I could move here when Fernando found me and told me about Nick and you being a target. I had to get to you after that. Fernando and Pedro are dealing with selling my house and other stuff now."

Wow. All Jessie's pretty words were exactly what she wanted to hear but she wasn't one hundred percent sure she could believe him yet. Kit's instincts were telling her he was telling her the truth, but she needed to give it some time to see if he truly was going to stick with her. And there was his work.

"What about your team?"

"Rallying is a global sport, Kit. I can be based anywhere... So Lutrec Racing is moving to Tasmania."

The sound of tires crunching gravel brought a sigh from Jessie as he loosened his hold on her. Reluctantly Kit pulled back from him and turned around to watch the others pull into the car park. Jessie took her hand in his as she walked over to where Jake was standing. It didn't take long for them all to gather in close. With two teams, there were a dozen of them plus Jake.

"Okay, listen up, everyone. Alex down at the station has been doing some discreet checks on Trigger for me. He's confirmed Trigger have people high up in the force. The first time someone saw him looking into Trigger Corporation he got pulled up and told to leave it alone as they had nothing to do with any of his current cases."

"Yeah, that doesn't sound suss at all."

Jake gave Xander a glare, but Kit had to agree with him.

"Alex saw it as the red flag it was. Further careful investigating shows Trigger Corporation owns a club in Hobart, the Classic Convicts."

Low groans filled the air.

"Sorry, Jake, it looks like everyone else knows that place by name but I have no clue."

Kit turned around to face Jessie, who was standing close to her back. "Classic Convicts is your usual inner-city bar, however the rear of the place is locally known as HoHaven. It's a strip club."

"Ah. Okay then."

With a chuckle, Jake began speaking again. "That's the one. Alex did a little snooping and has discovered that lately the place is at its busiest after closing time. It's never been like that before. The more Alex looks into this current little crime wave we're having, the more he thinks Trigger is behind it. While the crimes are small, more annoyances than anything harmful, there is never any evidence. Normally the type of people who run around doing graffiti on homes and stealing rubbish bins and bikes get caught quickly because they are careless. These guys are not. They are careful and leave nothing behind."

The sound of a vehicle approaching had them all watching the car park's entrance. Kit held herself still and tensed her muscles until she saw the blue Suzuki.

"Relax, it's only Sophie. Not sure why though."

Kit felt Jake's worry and kept her gaze fixed on the vehicle as it pulled to a stop. Sophie wasn't alone. Kit held her breath as the car doors opened; she wasn't sure what to expect. However, Jessie barking out a laugh as he ran forward was definitely not it. As the man who'd traveled with Sophie turned toward them, she relaxed. It was Jessie's friend Pedro.

"Pedro, *amigo*! I didn't know you were coming."

Sophie stepped around the two men and made her way over to Jake.

"Jessie had given him our house number. He rung to say he was flying out here for a visit. We thought it would be a nice surprise to not tell Jessie about it. Gee, guys, stop looking so worried. He knows exactly who we all are so you can still go for your run."

"But he's not one of us."

Xander once again voiced what they were all no doubt thinking, and Jessie turned to respond.

"Pedro has been my closest friend for years. I was the only one I knew who could shift forms. It got to the point I had to confide in someone about it all. Pedro had already shown himself worthy of my trust, and has continued to prove it many times since."

A familiar scent she hadn't smelled in a very long time floated over the breeze along with several others she didn't recognize and her blood ran cold. *Fuck.* A few of the others cursed and growled. Kit's heart sped up until it felt like it would beat out of her chest. She spun around and dropped into a fighter's stance just as a group of about twenty men emerged from the bush to surround them.

"What do you want?"

Jake's voice was strong, loud and laced with a growl that would have had any normal man running for cover. However, these were not normal men. They all wore shirts with Trigger's logo.

"You, of course. And the others. I think I'm heading for a promotion if I manage to bring in the alpha and his mate. Make it quick men!"

As they descended on them, Kit took a slow, deep breath and found her center. Pushing aside all emotion, she prepared to fight for her life, and those of her family. The first man to have at her was a cocky little shit. He wouldn't have been more than twenty years old. Stupid fool gave her a sly once over before he ran at her. When he got to her, he attempted to swing a haymaker punch at her head. Kit raised both arms to deflect the blow with her forearms then she quickly delivered a hand knife shot to the side of his neck. Fool went down from just one blow.

"Moron."

"You think you're an expert or something, doll?"

With a snarl, Kit spun to the next idiot. At least this one was in a fighter's stance. However, he was also bouncing around like a freaking kangaroo high on caffeine. Kit didn't move as he closed in. No point in wasting energy trying to chase him down. Let him wear himself out a bit as he made a big show of approaching her.

Finally he finished dancing around and moved in on her. She saw him shift his stance moments before he spun with a high kick. Kit was fast in delivering her own roundhouse. Straight to his exposed groin. Kneeling on the ground whimpering as he cupped himself, Kit delivered a final hard kick to the side of head, knocking him out cold.

"Fuck."

An arm came around her neck and pinned her back against a hard body. She gripped on to his arm as he turned with her to face yet another Trigger. She clenched her muscles as she saw the fists coming at her. With her abdomen rigid like it was, she barely felt the blows. She grinned as her attacker growled at her in frustration. Grabbing at the hand that was around her neck, she pulled back his little finger as she threw her head back, smacking him in the face. His grip loosened and she spun free of his hold, delivering a hard sharp elbow to his cheek as she did. Wasting no time she glanced over her shoulder as she executed a spinning kick that landed against the other man's chest before he could land another shot.

"Melina."

Terror and fear froze Kit's body in place as that single word was growled. Her lungs refused to work as she slowly turned toward the deep voice she'd know anywhere.

"No."

Her hoarse whisper was cut off when she was again grabbed around the throat and dragged backward. Kit was too stunned to effectively fight back. Two more men began laying punches and kicks into her as she was held immobile. She clenched her body but her arms and legs weren't responding to her commands. Her gaze never left him, even as her world clouded with agony.

Her father had found her.

Chapter Eight

Terror had Jessie on edge. He could hold his own in a bar fight, but he sure as hell wasn't a trained fighter like some of these other guys were. So far he'd managed to take down a couple. He'd glanced over at Kit early to see her kicking everyone's butt so he focused back on his own issues.

Suddenly pain gripped his heart hard, similar to what he'd felt when he'd found his mother lying dead in her bed. Certain the emotion was coming from Kit, he turned to look for her. Kit was holding herself rigid as Triggers pinned her back while others beat her. Without conscious decision, he roared and shifted. As the blue light cleared from his vision, he found two Triggers in front of him. Desperation gave him strength and he lunged at the men. He gripped one around the biceps with his claws as he bit into his shoulder. In one smooth move, he pulled his hind legs up and kicked into the guy's middle, tearing flesh free with his two-inch long claws. He allowed the dead man to drop to the ground as the other Trigger attempted to get him in a headlock. Didn't the guy know how strong snow leopards were? *Idiot*. With ease he swiped out a paw and clawed the side of his face. With a scream, he pulled away from Jessie while clutching at his bleeding face. *Yeah, that's going to leave a scar.*

With that dealt with, he turned back to Kit just in time to see another leopard go to her aid. It pulled the man off her back by the throat and lunged for the next one. Jessie raced over to help and was still feet away when one of the men buried a blade in the leopard's shoulder. The animal howled and fell to the ground allowing Jessie space to jump over it with a roar. He landed at the same time as another larger leopard joined him, roaring loud enough that Jessie felt it vibrate through the earth. The few remaining Triggers turned tail and ran at the sound. Jessie went to give chase but was stopped by Jake's voice in his head.

No Jessie. Not today. Our wounded need to be taken care of first. Sophie is going to need to go to hospital with that knife wound.

Oh shit. That was Sophie who had protected Kit? Jessie made his way back to Kit's side. She knelt on the ground silently staring off into the bush where the Triggers had gone. Her complete stillness scared him. The only movement was her chest rising and falling to breathe. Jessie returned to human form and was tossed a pair of jeans by another of the men.

"We all keep a spare set or two in our cars. Never know when you're gonna shift and shred your clothes."

"Good move. Thanks."

With his heart in his throat, he quickly dressed before he dropped to his knees in front of Kit and held her face in his palms.

"*Reinita*?"

He winced at the blood and bruises on her face and body. She'd taken a hell of a beating. Gently, he forced her face around until she looked into his gaze. Her eyes looked a little glassy for a moment before she blinked and hissed in a breath. Without a word, she shook her head and pulled free of him with a grimace and crawled over to Sophie's side. Jake was back in human form but was shaking and way too pale.

"Someone call Adele!"

Kit's voice was strong and confident as she called out while stroking the fur on Sophie's face.

"Already done, Kit. She's on her way." Xander seemed to be always calm and level headed, and Jessie wondered what it would take to rattle the man.

"We can't stay out here. They'll regroup quickly and return to finish the job."

Kit's voice had lost some of its harsh edge, and Jessie could see she was struggling to hold herself together. What the hell had happened that changed the fight? Kit had been expertly plowing through them one minute then that pain he'd felt from her kicked in and she seemed to be unable to fight at all. A quiet groan pulled him from his thoughts and he looked over at Jake.

"Jake doesn't look too good." Jessie wasn't sure why no one else had noticed how ill he appeared.

Xander glanced from Jake to Jessie. "He'll be fine, Jessie. Jake is a strong empath. He gets ill when he's surrounded by so many other people feeling strong emotions, add to that his mate being in agony with a knife wound... and yeah, he's going to be feeling pretty crappy for a while. Adele will be here soon with an ambulance. She'll take him with Sophie."

Jessie stood watching as Xander set about dividing up everyone into the cars and sending them all off to the hospital. It had been a nasty fight and it looked like they'd all sustained a few blows. A chill ran up his spine when he realized who was missing.

"Where's Pedro?"

"Relax, *amigo*."

Jessie spun around to face his friend, his uninjured and completely intact friend.

"How'd you escape?"

"Easy. I shoved him into Sophie's car as soon as I sensed the Triggers were here. He was a good boy and kept his head down so they didn't see him."

Pedro blushed as Xander explained.

"Just for the record, I do know how to fight."

Xander chuckled darkly. "Not against Triggers you don't."

Xander gave Pedro's shoulder a quick squeeze before he turned back to the others.

"Kit, why don't you head back in Sophie's car with Jessie?"

Kit snarled at Xander, "I'll take my bike. You know better than to say otherwise, Xander."

The big man crossed his arms over his chest as he

glared down at her. "You're injured, Kit. I'm not being a bastard here. You get on that bike, you'll come off."

Kit rose from Sophie's side and stalked up to stand in front of Xander. "No one rides my baby but me. And I'm not leaving it here for Trigger to take. I got a little roughed up, that's all. You know as well as I do that I'll be back to one hundred percent in no time."

"You still need to go to the hospital-"

"Where else would I be, Xander? I see Sophie as my mother and she's injured. *Because of me.*"

Jessie couldn't stand the strain in Kit's voice. He moved toward her but stopped when she turned on him. Her gaze was hard and cold. She'd put up a wall that no one was getting through.

"I'll take Sophie's car and follow her in, Xander."

Xander let lose a small growl, "You take it slow, Kit. You're not healed yet so don't try anything stupid." Kit marched over to Jake's car and with jerky movements retrieved her helmet and jacket as the ambulance pulled up near Sophie. Xander turned to Jessie.

"You need to keep a close eye on her, Jessie. Something happened and she's closed herself off. I haven't seen her go this cold since she was a teenager."

Jessie cursed in his head. Kit had finally allowed him to apologize and they'd been making some headway only an hour ago. Now he didn't know where he stood. Jessie desperately wanted to get Kit alone so he could attempt to break through that wall of hers before she had a chance to reinforce it. As he watched Sophie shift to human and be loaded into the ambulance, he doubted that was going to happen anytime soon.

Kit knew she was driving everyone nuts, but she couldn't muster up the energy to care at the moment. Three days later and she was still reeling that her father was part of Trigger Corporation and had done nothing to stop the attack on her. She knew his skills. After all, he'd been the one who had taught her most of what she knew about fighting. Kit wondered how long he'd been a part of Trigger. Had he already been a member prior to her shifting that first time? He'd loved her, had treated her like a princess, then in a moment on that morning it had all vanished—but she couldn't wrap her mind around him hating her enough to join Trigger so he could hunt her down.

Jessie and Jake had both tried to talk to her about what happened to make her freeze up in the fight like she had, but she couldn't admit it to them. Jessie knew more about her childhood than anyone else, but that was because he'd seen it in her dreams. She couldn't bring herself to voice the cold, hard truth, that just as she feared, her father had come after her. With a shudder, Kit realized that was the reason behind Trigger targeting her recently. It was because her father had finally tracked her down. She wondered where her mother was. Was she involved with Trigger too? An image of her mother's grief-stricken face on that final morning flashed through her mind for a moment. Had her father convinced her to hate their daughter too?

Feeling on edge and unable to sit still, Kit left Jessie and Jake in her lounge room to go get changed into her workout gear. Even the process of changing into her sports top and tight workout pants helped calm her. Walking barefoot, as she strapped up her hands, she made her way out to her back veranda. With her knuckles protected, she approached her punching bag and began working it over, landing kicks and punches against the black fabric until she could feel her muscles burn from the effort. With each strike against the bag, her mind loosened and cleared. Her thoughts made more sense and she began to process what had happened. Her own father was leading the way to take her out, but he wasn't the overall leader. Another Trigger had spoken when Jake confronted them, and he'd mentioned taking Jake and Sophie in had been their aim. Her father had to be of some importance though. It was the only way he could have been able to stand back from the fight like he had. Maybe there was a power struggle at the top? She could see her father not caring about taking out the alpha if he could get his chance to get his hands on her. It was obvious he'd been watching her, and for some reason grew tired of observing her. Had she shown poor form? She'd held her stances perfectly, executed every punch and kick with speed and power.

Kit growled at herself. *I don't need his approval. I've never needed his damn approval.* She continued to lay into the bag imagining what it would be like to pound into her father. She doubted he realized her full power and potential even after the fight. Man, what she wouldn't give to have a chance to show her old man what she could do.

A sharp bark brought her head up and her attention back to reality. Kelly sat on one of Kit's deck chairs with her head cocked to the side as she watched Kit intently. Raksha had found a tennis ball and was trying to get Kelly to take it from his mouth, obviously looking for a game of fetch.

"Hey, kiddo. Sophie drop in with you?"

"Yep. She's inside with the others. You know, you're really good at that."

Kit couldn't help but chuckle at the young teenager.

"I should be. Been doing it for about fifteen years now."

"Could you show me?"

Kit jerked in shock. Kelly had been abused, beaten to within an inch of her life. Kit hadn't thought the girl would ever want to know anything about violence. To be honest, she was rather surprised to find Kelly out here watching her by choice.

"Why'd you want to learn how to beat up a bag, kiddo?"

Kelly grabbed up the ball to throw for Raksha before she stood and walked over to Kit.

"I don't ever want to be a victim again. I heard Jake and Sophie talking about you, how good you were in that fight. I want to be like you. I want to be able to fight so well no one will ever pick on me again."

Tears welled in Kit's eyes. She'd had a soft spot for Kelly from the moment she'd met her. But that was because of what she'd been forced to survive. This warrior side of Kelly was something Kit had not seen before, and she liked it. Kelly was going to grow into such a strong woman, and Kit was more than happy to help her.

"I'm proud of you, Kelly, and I'd love to teach you how to defend yourself."

Leaning his head back against the couch, Jessie closed his eyes with a quiet sigh. He was tired. Since the fight, he'd been staying at Kit's place. Not that she'd noticed. He slept on her couch so he was able to monitor who came and went from her house. Kit's head wasn't in a good place. Since Sophie's release from hospital hours after the fight, she'd not spoken to anyone. The fact Jake was so worried about her didn't help ease Jessie's mind. How the hell could they get her to open up?

"Well, would you look at that!"

Jake's awed tone had Jessie opening his eyes and leaning forward to follow the older man's gaze. A smile tugged at his lips as he watched Kit and Kelly through the glass. They had Kelly's dalmatian bouncing around them like the crazy puppy it was.

"Kelly asked me on the way over if I thought Kit would show her some moves. Apparently she heard Jake and me talking about how great Kit was in that fight and it's added to her hero worship. That girl has always idolized Kit."

Jessie responded to Sophie without needing to think about it, "That makes sense. Kit's a warrior, a fighter. She's strong and basically no one messes with her because of her reputation. I can understand why a girl with Kelly's background would want that. She'd love the idea of being so tough she'd rarely have to actually physically prove it."

"You have a point, Jessie. And it will be good for both of them, training together. Kit gets stuck inside her head so much. She's never said much about her past, even to me or Sophie. But you know when she's hurting, because she always takes it out on that bag of hers."

Jessie stayed silent as Kit showed Kelly a blocking move before allowing the teenager to have a go using the move on Kit.

"Wonder how long since Kelly joined in?"

"Not sure, it's been about an hour since she headed out there, but last time I looked she was just sitting back watching."

Jessie only half heard the conversation continue between Jake and Sophie as he rose to go over toward Kit. She was so beautiful. He loved to watch the way her muscles flexed and moved as she shifted around the punching bag and play fought with Kelly. Obviously their lesson for the day was finished now and Kit laughed as she sparred with Kelly, pretending the young teen's hits were mortal wounds.

She glanced over to him and froze when she saw him watching her. He chuckled a little as her face reddened. Damn, she was adorable when she showed her soft feminine side. He swung open the door.

"You two having fun?"

"For sure, Jessie. Aunty Kit is the best. But I'm stuffed. What have you got to drink, Aunty Kit?"

Kelly wrapped an arm around Kit's and basically dragged her back into the house.

"Ahh, I think there's some juice in the fridge. Maybe some lemonade, if you're lucky."

"Cool."

With the information she wanted, Kelly was off, leaving Kit standing in front of him looking so damn lost his chest ached. He cupped her cheek with his hand, and she closed her eyes as she nuzzled into his palm with a soft sigh. He leaned in and pressed a light kiss to her forehead before he pulled away and took her hand to lead her over to the couch. He attempted to tug her to sit on his lap but she, of course, resisted. She did take the spot next to him so he wasn't too upset. It was the closest she'd let him be since those precious few moments before the fight.

Jake cleared his throat and waited for Kit to look at him. The moment she turned to face him, he spoke.

"Kit, we need to talk about what happened. I've always let you hold your secrets, but now I can't. Who was that man who called out 'Melina'? And who is she?"

Jessie was close enough to Kit that he saw her shudder

and stiffen. Instinct demanded he comfort her and he wrapped his arm around her waist and pulled her over so her body was flush against his. She held herself rigid but thankfully didn't pull away from him.

"My birth name is Melina Silva and that man was Gabriel Silva. My biological father."

Kit's words dropped like a bomb. The room went deathly silent. Jessie thought back to Kit's dream he'd seen, the one of her fifteenth birthday. She'd been very scared of her father.

"I always thought your birth name was different. Why Kit?"

Kit sighed as she pulled her legs up and curled her arms around her knees. "When you found me, you both referred to me as kitten. I liked how it made me feel. I couldn't be Melina anymore. I had to let that girl go and become someone new. I figured a new name would help."

"And how does your father fit in with the need for a new identity? Was he part of Trigger even back then?"

"Honestly, Jake. I don't know. I doubt it. After he saw what I could change into, he kicked me out with the threat that he'd kill me if he saw me again. If he'd been part of Trigger Corp, he would've simply done the job then and there."

Jessie wasn't so sure. Gabriel could have given his daughter one chance to get away and live her life.

Jake scrubbed his hands over his face. "Well, I guess that explains why you've been a target with them."

"It's my fault they're here. He's been searching for me, no doubt using his contacts. He was a police detective, no idea if he still is. Sophie getting hurt is on me. If I'd not come here, stayed here, Trigger Corp wouldn't have come. Nick would still be alive."

Kit's voice was hoarse with emotion, and Jessie knew she was trying to hold back tears. In one swift move, he wrapped her up in his arms and cradled her on his lap. She pressed her face into his neck and his heart ached as he felt her hot tears against his skin.

Jake looked around as he walked into Classic Convicts. He'd wanted to do this little recon visit last weekend, but after the attack there was no way he would leave Sophie. A full week later, she was as good as new. Jake was eternally grateful the knife hadn't caused any major damage and with her shifter genes she was now back to her normal self. So here he stood with Xander, Dominic, Jordan, Joel and Sean in their enemies' apparent hideout.

"How about we grab a beer at the bar and settle into a booth for a while, boys."

Classic Convicts was fairly busy, and Jake guessed that was usual for a Friday night. The place didn't look like anything special, but it was at least clean. He led the way to the bar with the others following. A young woman strolled up to serve them. Her hair intrigued him. It was a lovely chocolate brown but the sides were cut short and were slicked back while the top was longer, maybe one or two inches, and had been styled into a mohawk. As she stopped in front of him with a smile that didn't reach her eyes, the overhead lights glinted off her nose ring and Jake couldn't help but grin back at her as his instincts told him she was pure and not part of Trigger.

"So, what can I get you boys?"

Her British accent was unexpected and Jake took a moment to respond.

"A jug of beer with six glasses. Thanks, love."

"Name's Rachel, not love, and that'll be eighteen dollars, thanks."

She had spunk. Holding back a smirk, Jake handed over the cash and watched her fill a jug and grab half a dozen glasses for them. Once they were lined up on the counter, she ran her gaze over the younger men, causing Jake to chuckle quietly. Shifter males were a good-looking breed. He heard her sharp intake of breath as he felt a blast of emotion from beside him. Rachel was still gripping a glass in her left hand, and there was a small ring on that third finger. *Damn it.* One of his boys just found their mate, and she was taken. He turned to see who and cursed again when he saw it was Xander. The man was huge. At six feet six, he towered over even Jake. He had wide shoulders and strong arms. With his cleanly shaven scalp and strong jawline, he was pure alpha male. Jake always suspected Xander would one day leave the leap to live a more solitary life. Some shifters were more in tune with their cat, and snow leopards were by nature solitary creatures.

Jake could see the tension in Xander's jaw, the only sign of the strain he was under. Poor bloke had been dreaming of his mate for five years, he finally finds her and she's off the market.

"Thank you, Rachel."

Jake broke the moment and the other men helped him herd Xander over to a booth with their drinks. The man clearly didn't want to leave the bar but eventually gave in and joined them. As they settled into a booth, Xander glared at him.

"That's my mate. Why'd you pull me away?"

"You didn't see her left hand?"

"Didn't look, it was her face I was watching."

"Looks like she's engaged, son."

"Fuck."

Jake's chest tightened in sympathy for Xander. He allowed his gaze to return to the woman behind the bar and tensed at what he saw. Xander obviously did too because he let loose a low growl. There was now a man standing to Rachel's side. He was being very hands-on with her and she didn't look happy about it, however she wasn't fighting him off.

"Can you hear what he's saying to her, Xander?"

Like Jake's increased empathy, Xander's hearing was very sensitive and Jake was fairly certain he could hone it into a direction to hear conversations at a distance.

"Yeah, I can hear the bastard. He didn't like the way she looked at me. Prick was watching her on the surveillance camera."

Jake put a palm on Xander's shoulder. "You can't go over and take her. I wish you could, but that's not how it works. She saw you, sensed something between you. Take it slow with her and you'll win her over. Engaged isn't married and if that's the owner of her ring—well, she doesn't exactly look real happy with him, does she?"

"No, she isn't. I saw the look in her eyes and it was as far from happy as you get. Fuck, the pervert sitting at the bar asked him why Rachel isn't on next door. Apparently she'll be over there real soon."

Xander growled, and Jake could see his body vibrate with rage as the man grabbed at Rachel's breast before shoving her away from him with a slap to the ass. Jake swallowed down the bile rising in his throat from feeling Xander's rage on top of his own. No woman should be treated in such a way.

"Just told her to go get changed. We need to go next door. If that asshole puts her up on stage, I'm taking her."

Jake sighed and took a swig of his beer. He couldn't tell Xander no, not when he felt like doing the same thing.

"We've got your back, son."

It's not how he'd want things to happen, but he could not ask Xander to watch his mate strip for other men. Especially when it seemed like she wasn't doing it by choice. Xander drained his beer before slamming the glass down.

"I'm out of here. I can't listen to him talk about my

mate like he is. Fucking asshole."

"Xander, it's too early to go next door. Especially if he's noticed her watching you. Look at the tattoo on his neck. He's a Trigger. My guess would be that's Rocco Ferri, the owner. Let's just chill here for a little and see what other information we can pick up in regard to Triggers, then we'll head on over to HoHaven. Rachel has to get changed before she'll go over there, so we have a little time."

Xander turned his cold stare on Jake and he couldn't help but feel ill at the level of malice pouring off the guy.

"I don't like this, Jake. Every instinct I have is screaming for me to go get her. But I'm not stupid. Those few Triggers who survived last week could be here and if they see us and see me start something with her, they're going to know who she is to me, and that won't end well for her. That said, if she's on that damn stage when we go in there, I won't be able to stop myself. We clear?"

"Clear as day, son."

They all settled back in the booth and it hadn't escaped Jake's notice that the other boys were silent. Xander was easily the biggest man in their leap and even though he was not alpha or future alpha, everyone respected him. Normally Xander was level headed and calm under any circumstance. Jake suspected his mate was about to change all that.

Xander's skin itched as he fought against his instincts demanding he take his mate and claim her. He glared at the door to HoHaven. Red leather with brass studs; he supposed it was meant to look luxurious. However, the big guy standing next to the door with his bulging arms crossed over his broad chest ruined any attempt to make it look classy. The man was dressed well enough, with a tight black t-shirt and dress pants, but the expression on his face made it clear he was nothing but a thug. Xander was beginning to understand Rocco was surrounded by nothing but sleaze-balls. How the hell had Rachel come to be caught up with him?

Xander growled under his breath, cursing himself for not going in search of her sooner. His parents had always told him to have patience and allow fate to decide when he met his mate. They'd assured him that shifters always found their mate when they needed each other the most. Xander admitted, at least to himself, what the other reason he'd not gone looking for her was. About a year after he'd first dreamed of Rachel, he'd heard her voice and knew instantly her accent was British. He'd never been to England and had no idea where to start searching for her if he did go. He was sure Jake could line up someone in a leap over there to help him, but that would only help if she was one of them. The fact she was engaged to a Trigger had Xander thinking that wasn't likely.

Xander rolled his shoulders in an attempt to ease his tension. He glanced around the bar, taking in what the other patrons were doing. He looked at the faces of all the men, looking for Triggers they'd fought against.

"Oi, Rocco. Who's on stage tonight?"

The older man still sitting at the bar caught his attention as he spoke to Rocco. Xander honed his hearing in on the conversation.

"Full bill of girls tonight."

"Don't jerk me around, Rocco. You know what I'm asking."

Rocco laughed. "Yes, your favorite is up later. I'd be fool to not put Bella Diamond up on center stage. Woman pulls every dime from the crowd when she's on."

"Pity you can't convince her to work seven nights a week."

"Well, while she's pulling in what she is, she doesn't need to. Thursday through to Sunday is all we both need to make enough dough from her hot little body."

The older man sighed, "And what a body it is. Lucky bastard."

"That I am, buddy. That I am. Speaking of which, I'd better go check on things. I'll see you in there later."

Xander turned to watch as Rocco left the bar and headed over to the red door.

"What was that about, son?"

Jake's serious tone brought his attention away from the bar's owner.

"The club's apparent favorite stripper 'Bella Diamond' is going to be on stage tonight. The way Rocco and that sleaze spoke of her, has me thinking Rocco's sleeping with this stripper."

"So you think it might be Rachel?"

Xander clenched his jaw tight as fury raced through him. He couldn't speak so he nodded at his alpha. Jake frowned at him for a moment before he spoke.

"Okay, let's go in then. We all know the score. Try to not cause any trouble. We need to learn more about everyone involved here before we make any moves, so if we see any of the Triggers from the fight, we're out of here. Understand?"

He took a deep breath and focused on calming his emotions.

"I'll do my best, Jake. But I was serious when I told you I'd take her if he puts her on stage."

Jake sighed but didn't say a word as he moved out of the booth and headed over toward HoHaven. Xander allowed Jake to take the lead and speak to the thug guarding the door.

"Haven't seen you blokes before."

"Yeah, we wanted to try somewhere new tonight. So, what's the go?"

"Ten dollar cover charge, twenty if you want to sit at the stage. There's rooms for private dances, or if you don't mind being watched, you can use one of the booths along the back wall." Xander bristled as the thug paused to run his gaze over each of them. "Rules are simple. So long as you keep buying drinks and tipping the girls, you won't have any issues. Start causing trouble, you'll get tossed out on your asses and banned."

"Fair enough."

Jake pulled his wallet free and handed the guy enough to cover all of them.

"We'll just hang back tonight. Maybe next time we'll get front row seats."

With a nod, the door opened and Xander held his breath as he struggled to maintain his composed expression. He didn't want to tip off this thug to his emotional state. If he found Rachel on that stage, he would redefine this idiot's definition of what trouble was. Once they passed the entrance, they faced a dimly lit staircase leading down.

"Guess it's in the basement. How classy."

Xander had to agree with Sean. The black peeling paint on the walls didn't inspire confidence in the quality of the place either.

"Let's get this over with."

As he spoke, Xander moved past the others to take the lead. The sooner they got in, the sooner they could leave. He didn't slow his stride as he pushed through the thick red curtain at the base of the stairs. Instantly the muted thumping music became intense. Xander winced as it assaulted his sensitive ears. He'd never liked eighties rock anthems. Damn, he wasn't going to be able to take this for long. He wished he had earplugs with him.

"Dad, we have to leave. Xander's not doing so well."

Xander shook his head at Dominic. "I'm not leaving until I find out if Rachel is on that fucking stage."

The song finished and Xander closed his eyes a moment in gratitude. The next song started slow, LL

Cool J's "Doin' It". This he could handle. He strode over to a booth along the back wall and settled against the padded seat. The others followed his lead and a moment later, a pretty waitress wearing a sparkly silver mini skirt and a tight black tank top that left her belly bare approached them. Xander let the others worry about drinks as he began to scan the club. It was relatively early so there were only about a dozen men here. He didn't recognize any of them as Trigger. He then turned his attention to the stage. It was in the shape of a T, with three poles along the back then another one at the end of the catwalk. All four were being put to good use by women who looked nothing like Rachel. He exhaled slowly, suppressing his relief for the moment. He couldn't be certain she wouldn't be on stage later.

"I'm here to serve drinks, not dance. You want to watch women taking their clothes off, turn your attention toward the stage, because I sure as fuck am not stripping back here for your—or anyone else's—entertainment."

With a grin, he turned toward the bar. He knew her voice and he adored her spunk.

"What's that grin for?"

"Because, Dominic. Rachel is tending the bar and she just told some joker to fuck off when he asked her to strip. No way does she work the stage. Not from what she just said."

"Yet Rocco spoke as though he knew at least one of the strippers intimately..."

Xander frowned as he mulled over Jake's words, his

heart aching for Rachel.

"What's the bet that fucker is cheating on her."

"I imagine it would be almost unusual for a strip club owner to not sample his staff."

Joel's quiet comment was followed by Xander's growl. He couldn't hold it back.

"Bastard doesn't deserve her."

Jake sitting up straight had Xander's full attention.

"And that boys, is our cue to leave. You good to go Xander?"

Xander followed Jake's gaze to a group of men who'd just entered. Three of the men were from their fight a week ago.

"Yeah, for tonight. Let's get out of here."

Chapter Nine

Jessie smiled as he stirred an aromatic mix of tomato, garlic and onion in a pot on the cooktop. He breathed in deeply, filling his senses with the aroma as he moved to the chopping board where he had pieces of fresh salmon ready to go into the sauce. Having always eaten a lot of seafood in Arica, Jessie was grateful Tasmania had a similar variety of fish available. He glanced across the room and winced as his heart jolted at the sight of Kit curled up on the couch, looking outside. She was still trying to keep herself safe behind her mental walls. It had been over a week since Kelly had managed to open her up a little and she'd admitted to Jake and him about her father. But she'd been silent on the matter since then, never uttering another word on the subject. She still insisted on going out on patrols but Dominic had put her on leave from firefighting. Kit hadn't liked being told she was a liability out in the field until she got her head on straight, but she hadn't been able to argue his perfectly valid points.

With a frown, he ran his gaze over her body and noted she'd lost weight. Her cheeks were sunken in more than they had been during the rally and her collarbones were more prominent too. He hoped he would be able to coax her into eating tonight. After adding the fish to the sizzling sauce, Jessie turned to the fridge to start preparing the salad.

It didn't take him long to have everything ready to eat and he grabbed some cutlery along with the two plates and made his way over to the couch. He set everything down on the coffee table before he pulled it closer to them. Kit hadn't moved from where she was blankly staring out the window. Her stillness bothered him more than the silence. When she was out in the world she pretended to be normal, but here in her home, she simply shut down and withdrew into herself. Jessie's heart ached for her. He could still feel her pain so knew the extent she was still suffering.

With a gentle palm, he cupped her cheek and turned her to face him before he brushed his lips over hers lightly.

"You need to eat, *reinita*. If you want to keep doing patrols, you need to keep your strength up." He brushed a thumb over the dark smudge under her eye. "And sleep. You're not getting enough."

His hand slipped from her face as she slowing uncurled and turned to face the plate he'd put down in front of her.

"Thanks, Jessie. It looks great, and smells even better."

Her voice was void of emotion, but at least she was attempting to communicate with him.

"No problem, Kit. I hope you enjoy it."

He began eating his own meal while he snuck glances at Kit to make sure she actually ate. To start with, she only moved the food around her plate. Finally she gave in and ate a mouthful. Once she started, she seemed to realize how hungry she was and devoured the entire meal in no time. Jessie hid his smile behind his fork as with a sigh, she relaxed against the couch.

"That was amazing, Jessie. Thanks again for cooking it. I know I haven't been great company lately and I'm sorry."

Jessie shrugged off her praise even as his chest swelled with pride that she liked his cooking.

"You've copped a rough time lately, I understand."

Unsure what else to say, he quietly finished off his food before he looked at her again. When he did, he found her fast asleep. He grinned at how sweet she looked. Kit was undoubtedly the most extraordinary woman he'd ever met, that was for sure. He quietly rose and slipped into her bedroom to switch on the bedside lamp and turn down the covers. He returned to her side and gently scooped her up in his arms so she rested curled against his chest. He purred a little at how right she felt in his embrace. After walking the short distance to her bed, he laid her down on the mattress before he took off her shoes and socks. She was wearing a loose t-shirt and soft comfy shorts so he didn't bother trying to strip her further. He simply tucked her in, and with a kiss against her temple, he left her to rest.

As Jessie set about cleaning up the kitchen, his heart felt a little lighter. She'd eaten a full meal and was now sleeping peacefully; it was certainly a step in the right direction. With a groan, he frowned at the couch. He really didn't want to sleep on that uncomfortable thing again. Before settling in for the night, he wandered down the hall to Kit's room to check on her to discover her whimpering and thrashing in her sleep. *Guess she's not sleeping so peacefully after all.* Toeing off his shoes and removing his socks and shirt, he slid onto the other side of Kit's large bed, staying on top of the covers.

"Shh, *reinita*. I'm here with you now. I'll keep you safe."

Without waking, she turned toward him, and he gladly wrapped her in his arms. Instantly she calmed and her breathing leveled out. Relief coursed through him as she accepted his comfort. Even if she was asleep and unaware of her actions, it was a step forward. He lowered his cheek to rest on the top of her head and took a deep breath, filling his senses with her scent before he closed his own eyes to attempt to get some rest.

Even before Kit opened her eyes, she'd known her room was brighter than usual. The morning summer sunshine streamed in through her open curtains. Why hadn't she shut them last night? As she blinked open her lids, her mind and body came online and she became aware she was not alone. Her lungs stilled as she focused on the man lying next to her. Jessie's deep, even breathing made it clear he was still fast asleep, so she propped herself up on an elbow and took a moment to really look at him.

He was lying on his back on top of the covers, still wearing his jeans, not that they took away from his masculine beauty. Jessie was one very well put together male. His light brown hair was a gorgeous mess and his strong jaw was covered in stubble. His alluring silver-blue irises were hidden behind his closed lids but the way his thick eyelashes fanned over his tanned flesh had her heart rate speeding up.

Following the line of his neck down to his broad shoulder, she couldn't help the small sigh that passed her lips. Her palm was resting against him, as though they'd slept entwined. She took in the way the slightly lighter skin tone of her hand looked against his smooth chest. Her fingers tingled from the heat radiating from his hard pectorals.

That hard block of ice she'd felt inside her since Jessie abandoned her after the rally was slowly melting, and she didn't feel cold anymore. She still felt torn up inside, guilt over Nick and Sophie, along with mortification that her father had truly tracked her down to take her out. But with Jessie here beside her, she felt somehow content. He truly was her mate, even without the ceremony. They were connected and she couldn't stand the thought of him being harmed because of her. She couldn't let on publicly what he meant to her. If her father caught wind of it, he'd not stop until Jessie was dead. Kit knew without a doubt

Gabriel was cruel enough to make her watch and live with the knowledge it was her fault—for at least a short while, before he'd end her life too.

"Don't cry, *reinita*, you're breaking my heart."

Jessie's large hands cupped her face as his thumbs wiped away tears she hadn't been aware of shedding. She shook her head, trying to clear her thoughts but as she looked into his worried silvery-blue gaze, she saw them dulled over with death and his skin covered with blood. With a panicked shriek, she flew from the mattress and pressed herself against the far wall. Her lungs didn't want to work, her breath sawed in and out of her throat as she blinked her eyes in an attempt to clear the image her imagination had produced.

Jessie was going to die.

Because of her, he would die.

"Kit? What's wrong? Talk to me. Tell me what's going on."

She shook her head, "Stay away from me. He'll hurt you. If he knows, he'll hurt you!"

Jessie slowly left the bed and prowled over to her.

"Who? And knows what?"

"Gabriel. If he knows what you are to me, he'll kill you for it."

Kit's skin felt overly sensitive. Her instincts were flaring and her mind was a mess. She could barely hear over the pounding of her heart and she saw the look in Jessie's eyes. He thought she was crazy.

"I need to go. I can't. Breathe..."

She turned and bolted out of the room. She ran through the house and slammed open her back door. She pulled her clothes from her body and gave over to her animal. Instantly she was surrounded by blue light as she shifted to her snow leopard. She heard Jessie on the phone to Jake as he ran behind her, and with a growl she scooped up her clothes in her mouth before she took off into the bush at the rear of her property. She needed to go for a run, clear her head. Maybe then she could work out how to save Jessie.

She headed out of Rosebery, deeper into the thick bush as she felt Jessie behind her. Damn it, he wasn't meant to follow her! She picked up speed in an attempt to lose him. She wove in and out of trees aimlessly running until the smell of a group of humans assaulted her nose. She slowed and sniffed the air. The scent was familiar; the Triggers from the fight were close by.

Kit, stop running. You know it's too dangerous for you to be alone at the moment.

Jake's commanding voice boomed through her mind. He was her alpha and had a lot of pull over her, especially when she was in animal form.

I've found their scent. Their base must be near here somewhere. I'm going to find it. I can sense Jessie and the others close by. I'm not alone, Jake.

I've sent both teams after you, Kit. You wait for them to join you before you go near any Triggers. Do you hear me, Kit? You. Wait.

They'd better hurry then, because I'm not waiting

more than five minutes.

She ended their conversation when she shifted and dressed, grateful she'd thought to grab her clothes. She slipped closer to where she'd sensed the group of men until she saw a house. It was a large stone building. There were a number of them around Tasmania, large homes built back in the days of convicts out on farms. This one looked to be in good condition. She'd bet the interior had been gutted and redone to include modern facilities. How many were in there? She sniffed the air but couldn't get a bead on how many. All she knew for sure was that her father was in there.

Dominic sat in the office at the firehouse and attempted to fill in the roster for the next month. Dammit, with so many shifters out on the patrols he was short on staff and it being summer, he needed to have the place fully manned. At least Conner was back on deck now that Tina was safe. He shoved his keyboard away as he reached for the ringing phone.

"Rosebery firehouse, Dominic speaking."

"Hey, son, I need you over at the farmhouse south of the lake. Kit's lost the damn plot and ran off on Jessie this morning. Now she's managed to stumble across her father."

His dad had filled Dominic in on the Trigger connection between Kit and her father, Gabriel, earlier in the week. This wasn't a good development at all.

"Shit. That isn't going to end well. Did she find just

him, or a group of Triggers?"

"I'm not certain. After Jessie rang to tell me, I shifted and sent out a mental order for her to stop running and she reported back that she thinks she's found their base. Damn woman. You know she's not going to wait for backup."

"Who have you sent to her?"

"Both teams."

"Okay, that's a dozen shifters, Dad. She'll be fine. But if you want I can head over there, so long as you come down here. We're short on firies already. I can't leave the crew without a captain."

"Yeah, okay. I'm on my way. I need you over there as alpha to keep things in control. If possible."

Dominic understood why he had to go. He'd noticed how as his father got older, he struggled more and more to deal with the aftermath of his heightened empathy.

"I'm leaving now."

"Stay safe, son."

"Always."

Dominic hung up and bolted from the room, nearly plowing into Conner.

"What's going on? I didn't hear the alarm go off."

"Dad rang. I've gotta go drag Kit's tail away from the fight of her life. He's on his way here to take over for me. You all right to hold the fort until he arrives?"

With his hands on his hips, Conner frowned. "Of course, Dom. But I'd rather come with you if Kit's in trouble."

"I know, brother, but you're needed here. Dad's already sent the teams to her location. I have to get moving. Talk to you later."

In no time, Dominic was gunning his trusty Rav 4 out of the car park and on his way to the lake. He pulled up alongside several other cars and jumped free to find a dozen of his men standing around watching as Jessie and Kit faced off against each other.

"What the hell is going on?"

All of them turned toward him, but Kit was the one who spoke.

"I want to go in and clean house but Jessie disagrees."

"Kit, you can't just run in and take them all out! You'll get yourself killed."

Jessie's voice was rough with frustration and fury. Poor bastard. Dominic had always known Kit's mate was going to be in for a hard time when he finally turned up. The woman gave stubborn a new name.

"Jake has sent me here in his place as alpha, so you *will* listen to me, Kit. Jessie's right. Going in there on your own is suicide." He raised his hand when she went to speak, "No, let me finish. We will be storming the house, but no one is going to be alone. We will plan and co-ordinate, then go in. Do you understand me? Because if you don't, I'll hogtie you if I have to, and we'll go do this without you."

Her gaze was as a hot as a wildfire but Dominic stood firm against it. Finally she rolled her shoulders and gave in.

"Okay."

The word was growled more than spoken and she wasn't at all happy with him, but at least she wasn't trying to make a run for it.

"All right, head count first..." Dominic quickly scanned them. "Fourteen with me. That's good. An even number. We go in pairs, and we all stay in our pairs. No one is to be caught alone." He paused to rub his face as he tried to think of how to best do this. "We don't want to get caught inside the house. Ideally, getting them out on the grass to fight will work in our favor. Give us room to shift if we need to and remove the chance of us being cornered into exposed positions. I've seen this place before and can tell you it only has two exterior doors, front and back. So, I say we split into two groups and call them out to us."

"One word from me and Gabriel will come running, and you know it. I doubt the other group will have to do a thing; the other Triggers will scramble to surround us. Some of them will come from around the back to try to sneak up on us."

Dominic rested his hands on his hips and glared at Kit in frustration. "You're out to make yourself a target today aren't you, little sister?"

"I won't be responsible for any more of my leap family being killed or injured. No one else is to take out Gabriel. That bastard is mine."

"Why, Kit? If you want us to leave one of these bastards who was there when Sophie was knifed alone, you need to give us a good damn reason."

Sean had moved toward Kit as he'd spoken. Dominic gave Kit a nod when she looked to him. She needed to tell them all this small part of her history.

"I wasn't born Kit Jones. My parents named me Melina Silva. That man, Gabriel Silva, is my father. He's been searching for me to take me out since I was fifteen. It's my fault he brought Trigger to us. Nick's death and Sophie's injury are on me, because of him. So he's mine."

"Wait, so Gabriel is a shifter too?"

"Some of you obviously haven't heard. Kit and Jessie are the South American Comet Shifter pair from the last passing." Dominic spoke up for Kit who looked incapable of speech. Jessie had her pulled against him as she hid her gaze from everyone.

"Okay, fair enough. Gabriel is yours."

Dominic gave Sean a slap on the shoulder as the man moved away from Kit.

"Right. The other point is that Gabriel is extremely well trained in martial arts. Do not engage him if you don't have to. You've all seen Kit in a fight, now you know who taught her."

A few muttered curses filled the air before they quieted down again.

"Kit? You ready for this, little sister?"

Dominic knew she was waiting for them all to abandon her. Her greatest fear was to be rejected. He'd known no one in their leap would ever do such a thing, but she hadn't been able to believe it.

Kit pulled away from the safety of Jessie's embrace. She'd hidden her face against him to escape her leap brothers' reactions to who she was. She didn't want to see their condemnation or rejection. After taking a deep breath and with her chin held high, she turned to scan all their faces. Her lungs froze as she saw respect and care in their gazes. Not one of them looked angry or upset with her. She swallowed past the lump in her throat before she looked back to Dominic.

"I'm ready to clean house. Let's get this done."

"Right, I'll join team one and we'll take the front while team two will take the rear. That'll put eight of us out front, six out the back. Before we go, Kit, you put a spare set of clothes in team one's vehicle didn't you? Because you're not really dressed for a fight."

Kit looked down at the shirt and shorts she'd slept in the previous night. She felt her cheeks heat as she dashed over to the SUV. Grateful its rear door opened to the side, she changed behind it quickly, leaving her feet bare, before returning. A buzz coursed through her and she couldn't stand still as she anticipated the upcoming fight. She was going to end this crap with her father once and for all.

"Right. Before we go in, I need to make this clear. We'll be taking lives today. Anyone not up for that needs to stay behind. If you hesitate for even a moment, they will kill you. These are the men who, in cold blood, killed Nick. They won't hesitate to do the same to any one of us. They also know who and what we are, so don't hesitate to shift. Everyone got the weapons they need?"

Kit glanced around as the men pulled various knives free from holsters attached to their belts to show Dominic. *Yep, my boys are armed alright*. She left her own knife sheathed on her hip, grateful she'd thought to put in a spare with her change of clothes. She knew the confrontation with her father would come to blows. Her pride and honor demanded she beat him on a level field with no weapons and in human form, but she also knew the value in having a backup plan, just in case he decided to fight dirty.

"All right, let's get this over with. Remember, Triggers have been wiping out leaps for a long time and know what they're doing. We have the element of surprise, but we're also on their home turf."

With all her senses on full alert, Kit jogged down the grassed road edge with the men. As they neared their target, the second team broke off into the bush to come up around the back. Kit loved how they just picked a team and divided up; Dominic didn't have to tell anyone where to be or which team to join. Just before they rounded the corner to where they would be able to see the house, Kit gasped in shock as Jessie grabbed her arm and hauled her against him for a hard fast kiss.

"Be careful, *reinita*."

The concern and care in his voice and gaze left her speechless. She nodded and pressed her lips to his once more before she pulled away and led them out into the front yard of the old house. She stood a couple yards back from the front door and glanced left and right to see Jessie and her leap brothers had formed a line behind her. Swallowing her fear and allowing the adrenaline to fortify her, she cleared her throat.

"I know you're in there, Gabriel! Come out and face me, you bastard."

She yelled the words and total silence followed her outburst. A nervous tingle raced over her skin as she waited for her call to be answered. After a minute, the front door slowly opened to reveal her father. He strolled out onto the front porch like he was going for a casual walk through a park. Five others followed him out, including the punk who'd tried to grab her at the rally.

"You want something, Melina?"

"Yeah, I want you and your lackeys gone."

A couple of the men bristled at her calling them her father's underlings. *Interesting, maybe he isn't as high up the food chain as I first thought.* She smirked as the punk who'd attempted to take her flicked his confused gaze between her and Gabriel.

"You two know each other?"

Kit smiled an evil malicious grin. "Didn't the mighty Gabriel Silva tell you? I'm his little girl, all grown up."

Gabriel growled as the other men all cursed and stepped away from him, like they might catch some disease from him that would turn their kids into shifters. *Idiots.*

"Enough! It doesn't matter, the moment you became

one of them, you ceased to be mine."

"I call bullshit, Gabriel. I've seen how you've been watching her."

With that comment, the young punk jumped down the few steps from the porch and began to sprint toward her. With a growl, Gabriel was a step behind him, which seemed to be the signal the others were waiting for as they too headed their way. Kit dropped back into a fighter's stance as all five Triggers headed straight for them. The punk made it to her first and she timed her spinning kick so it would land hard against his chest. As predicted, the impact knocked him off his feet to her left where Jessie launched himself at the downed man, allowing Kit to focus on Gabriel, who was eyeing her up and down as he came closer.

"You honestly think you can take me, Melina?"

"Yeah, I do. So quit talking and come get me."

He laughed at her as he shook his head. "You were always so cocky, Melina. It will be your downfall, that over-confidence of yours."

She focused on his body movements, ignoring his words. He was circling her, with his hands down by his sides. He looked relaxed at a glance, but she knew he was preparing to strike. Trying to find her weakness.

The sounds of shouts and flesh hitting flesh were loud around her but she pushed it all aside and stayed honed in on Gabriel. She knew Jessie would watch her back while she handled him.

Finally he passed close enough to her to lash out with

a thigh kick. The moment he shifted his weight to his back leg he gave away his intent. Kit lunged forward, placing her leg close to his to block the blow. She barely felt the impact of his knee against hers as she followed through with a solid one-two punch to the center of his chest. He raised his arms to block her but she was too fast for him and he stumbled back a step or two at the impact of her fists.

"Got faster reflexes than you, old man. And I know all your moves."

With a curse, Gabriel dropped into a fighter's stance and went on the attack without wasting a moment. Kit blocked his rapid punches and kicks as he blocked hers. She felt the sweat trickle down her back as the fight continued. Her father might be getting on in years, but he'd clearly kept up his training. However, that didn't stop him from tiring. When his fists lowered away from his face, she took advantage and lashed out with a fast heel-palm shot to his nose. He turned his head but she still caught him hard over his cheekbone. He threw out his leg and caught her in the side of her knee before she could move out of the way. She stumbled to her knees, but didn't let it keep her down. She turned toward him and landed a rapid one-two punch to his thigh and knee. He dropped down with a curse as she bounced back up to her feet and landed a solid front kick against his chest, which sent him sprawling onto his back in the dirt.

"Told you I could take you, old man." She pressed her boot over his throat as she continued to speak. "Where's

Mum? She in that house?"

"No, Camila left about six months after we kicked you out. She missed you and blamed me when she couldn't find you. She changed her name and moved away, searching everywhere for you. I kept tabs for a while but eventually I stopped looking. She made it clear she didn't want to ever see me again."

A small burst of joy lit inside Kit. Her mother had gone looking for her. Suddenly her world tilted. Gabriel had taken advantage over her lapse in concentration and threw her leg around so, in order to prevent her leg being broken, she spun over and landed face first on the dirt. She reared back, and looking over her shoulder, kicked back at him. He dodged her leg, avoiding the hit but it didn't matter, it gave her precious seconds to get back to her feet and face him. She locked her emotions up tight and focused on ending this.

Chapter Ten

It hadn't taken long for Jessie to realize just how well Triggers were trained. He needed every one of his instincts on full throttle to keep his head, so he took a step away from his opponent to shift to his snow leopard. The blue haze cleared from his vision to reveal a man coming straight for him, knife in hand. Jessie growled and ducked, the blade aimed at his head. The idiot put so much force behind his swing that he spun around and gave Jessie his back before he could catch himself. On reflex, Jessie pounced on him, swiftly landing him face first in the dirt. Wasting no time, Jessie wrapped his jaws around his neck and bit down until he heard a crunch and the body beneath him stilled.

Refusing to focus on the life he just took, Jessie leapt free and instantly began searching for Kit. He stilled when his gaze found her. She'd just sprung up from the ground to face off against Gabriel. They both had dirt and blood all over them from their fight, and he noticed that Kit's knife still hung from her belt untouched. He moved to go help her when Dominic's voice stopped him.

No, Jessie. Not yet. Kit will never forgive you if you take this from her.

He wanted to scream. He knew Dominic was right, but he hated not being able to run in and save her from having to do this. Jessie knew firsthand how having to put down your father affected you. He didn't want that for her, especially when he was here and capable of taking care of it for her. In an effort to distract himself, he glanced around the yard and saw that all thirteen shifters were there. Five leopards, eight men. Obviously no Triggers went out the back and team two had moved in to help them. Everyone looked a little battered but they'd all survived the battle.

Is it over? Aside from Gabriel.

Yes, the house has been searched and all the Triggers have been disposed of.

Jessie turned back to Kit as he tried not to focus on the fact that yet again, he was sidelined while she fought. He watched as she traded kicks and punches with her father. She was clearly stronger and faster than the older man, but he wasn't giving up. He was obviously well trained and highly skilled. He feigned a low kick and as Kit prepared to block it, he gripped her shoulder to hold her still for him to land a solid elbow strike to Kit's jaw. Gabriel followed it up with a knee to her stomach before she tore free of his grip and staggered back. Jessie growled and stepped forward. No way in hell would he stand here and simply watch his woman get taken down. She'd probably hate him for interfering, but he'd deal with that later. Better she be alive and pissed off than dead. Before he made it more than a handful of steps, Kit was back in her father's face.

"Cheap shot, old man. And I'm done with your crap."

Almost faster than Jessie could track, Kit pulled her knife free and buried it to the hilt in her father's chest before she stepped away from him, her calm gaze never leaving her father's. Shock filtered over Gabriel's features as he tried to grip the handle with his now uncoordinated hands, but in seconds he was on the ground, dead. Jessie was more than a little shocked as he watched Kit, with complete calmness turn to look around the yard.

"We all done here?"

"All the Triggers have been dealt with, yes."

She nodded at Sean's answer, "Good."

Without looking at anyone in particular, Kit turned and walked away. Jessie didn't know what to do. The others had all shifted to human form and had begun clean up. He whined as his heart ached for her while his mind refused to come up with a plan.

"Go watch over her, Jessie. I know she realizes there was no choice, but that man was still her father and the one who raised her. Can't imagine what she's feeling right about now."

Jessie winced as he shifted back to human. He held Dominic's gaze a moment as he tried to decide whether he should tell the man his biggest secret. In the end, he figured Dominic would one day be his alpha so needed to know.

"I know exactly how she feels, Dominic. Although, I

was only fifteen when I was forced to take my father's life."

Dominic's eyes grew wide for a moment before he swallowed and smoothed his expression out with a small nod of his head.

"Dad thought there was a skeleton in your closet you weren't talking about. You ever want to discuss it with me in detail, I'm here for you, but today's not the day to do it. This mess is going to be a bitch to clean up and it's going to take time."

He glanced around at the dead Triggers lying in the yard.

"How exactly are you going to deal with the bodies?"

"Go deep into the bush and dig a really big hole. We'll toss the bodies and their stuff in, then set them alight to destroy anything that will lead back to us. After that, we bury the remains, followed by a burn off around it. That way it's reported to the authorities as a grass fire and there's no question about the smoke seen or the disturbance to the ground. Not to mention it also allows us to close off the area so no one will pick up on the smell of burning flesh."

Eying the man suspiciously, Jessie had to ask.

"You say that like you've done it before?"

Jessie wasn't sure if he should be concerned.

"Nah, this is a first for me. Dad's had to do it a time or two in his lifetime as alpha. As future alpha, I get to learn all these charming tricks. Now, grab yourself a pair of pants from inside and go after your mate, hopefully before she does something stupid or reckless."

Nudity didn't really bother Jessie, but at the same time he didn't want to be jogging around town in his birthday suit. He quickly dashed into the house and grabbed a pair of shorts from a bag in a bedroom. He pulled the slightly too-large things on before he rushed up the road toward where they'd left the cars near the lake. He found Kit standing at the lake's edge. She'd rolled up her pants and had her feet in the water.

"Go home, Jessie. I need to be alone right now."

He rubbed the skin over his aching heart. Damn but rejection stung every time.

"I don't think that's a good idea, Kit. You shouldn't be alone after what you were forced to do."

"You don't have to stand guard, Jessie. I'm not going to do anything stupid like Dominic no doubt warned you I would. I need my space, that's all, especially now."

Frustration mixed with his fear for her and caused him to lash out before he could think better of it.

"You have a special way of making me feel like a useless bloody shadow, Kit. I know better than anyone you don't need a damn guardian. Every time I find you, you're kicking someone's ass and saving the fucking day all on your own!"

When Kit turned on him with fire in her gaze, his brain stuttered mid-thought, while his breath froze in his lungs. She stormed over to him with clenched fists until they stood toe to toe.

"You're damn straight I don't need a fucking guardian,

and I certainly don't need a damn shadow. I need a mate. Someone strong enough to stand beside me, not some boy who follows me around bitching all the damn time."

With a growl and flash of teeth, Kit spun around and stormed off toward the vehicles as Jessie's own temper flared to life.

"There's no damn room at your side for me, Kit!"

He saw her shake her head moments before she ducked behind the rear door of a car, stripped and shifted. Shaking with his anger and frustration, he watched her beautiful sleek snow leopard disappear through the heavy bush. With a growl, he spun around and kicked a pile of stones into the lake. Damn woman was going to drive him insane!

Dominic had known Kit for long enough to know that she kept her pain hidden deep inside, and the chances of Jessie being flayed by her tongue were high. He made sure to make enough noise on his approach that Jessie knew he was coming. He was sure, like him, Jessie's instincts were still flaring after the fight and he really didn't want to have to fight off the man if he went on the attack before he realized it was him, not a Trigger.

"Hey, Jessie. Guess Kit's already taken off home. Let me give you a lift."

Dominic knew as well as Jessie did that it would be quicker for him to jog through the scrub to Kit's place, but the bloke looked frustrated, lost and angry. Jessie slammed his way into Dominic's Rav 4 without a protest.

As Dominic put the SUV in gear and reversed out onto the road, he started talking.

"You know, I've known Kit for over ten years now. She's always kept a lot of secrets but her heart is pure. She's put herself on the line time after time for her leap family without hesitation. But she's never let anyone do the same for her. I can't think of a single time where she's stood back to let someone go in to bat for her, even as a teenager." He chuckled a little as he recalled how hotheaded she'd been as a teen. "*Especially* as a teenager."

Jessie sighed loudly as the poor bloke stared out the window.

"What the hell am I doing? Kit doesn't want me in her life, and she certainly doesn't need me. I should never have moved here. It was a mistake to think that this whole predestined mate thing was anything but a bloody fairytale."

Dominic winced at the pain in Jessie's tone. He turned up a road that would take them to a look out over the top edge of the lake where he knew it would be quiet and they could have a long chat.

"When I first met my mate, Adele, she didn't want anything to do with me. She was raised by a broken-hearted single mother, and she'd been brought up to firmly believe she didn't need a man in her life, because all a man would do is break a girl's heart before leaving. Didn't help that Adele was also grieving the loss of her mother to cancer. When Adele first came to

Rosebery for a job interview, she seemed to not need anyone either. She'd become a qualified nurse and paramedic on her own. My mate is so damn headstrong and independent I had trouble even getting her attention, let alone managing to get close enough to hold a conversation with her. Trust me, more than once I wondered if I'd ever manage to claim her."

"What happened? How did you end up becoming a vital part of her world?"

Dominic pulled up the car and switched off the engine before turning to Jessie with a grin.

"Persistence and kindness, my friend. This predestined mate thing, it's not a bunch of made-up bullshit. Just like me and Adele, you and Kit were born for each other. The reason you're perfect for one another is not because some higher power pointed at you both and said so. It's because you were quite literally made for each other. Your personalities complement each other, and you feel a pull to be near her, to protect her. And between the sheets, epic just doesn't cover it.

"Eventually, with me continually being around her she gave in and agreed to go on a date with me. It was while we were hiking that first time when we stumbled across Kelly. Poor kid had been beaten to within an inch of her life before she'd escaped. That girl was in bad shape. The way Adele cared for that poor abused child melted my heart and I knew then I loved her. For her, not because I'd been told I was meant to. She ran herself into the ground looking after Kelly and keeping her safe. We had no idea who'd hurt her or if they'd try to collect her, so I called in the cats and we set up a schedule to guard Kelly's hospital room. Kit took a lot of shifts."

Dominic paused to rub the back of his neck. He couldn't believe it had been less than a year since all that went down.

"While Adele is a strong and capable woman, she needed someone to take care of her. I had to make sure she ate, slept—remembered to take time out for her, not just Kelly. These shifter women of ours have a tough exterior and are strong as nails but they're still soft and fragile inside. They tend to put everyone else above their own needs and happily allow themselves to suffer. Kit does need you, Jessie, just as you need her. I doubt either of you realize just how much yet."

"Yeah well, that tough exterior Kit has must be made out of kryptonite or something. Because no matter what I try to do, it won't crack."

Dominic's heart ached for both Jessie and Kit.

"Give it time, Jessie. Out of necessity Kit had to become self-sufficient at a young age, as I'm guessing you did too. It'll take some time and a lot of patience, but you'll get there. You both feel the draw to each other, and that's clear to anyone who sees you together. She was forced to take her father's life today. I suspect he is the reason behind a lot of the secrets Kit's kept from the leap for all these years. To take a guess, I'd say her emotions are going to be pinging all over the place for a while."

Dominic started the Rav and began to head toward

Kit's place.

"She's going to need you more than ever. So, I need to ask: Where's your head at? You sticking with her or leaving for Chile?"

Jessie heaved in a deep breath as his thoughts continued to run wild. He glanced over at Dominic. Jessie hadn't known the man long, but he felt a kinship with him, especially after hearing that even though he was the future alpha of the leap, he had still had trouble capturing his mate.

"The reason I left the first time was because I was scared I'd ruin Kit. She's so innocent and pure, while I'm a murdering playboy."

Dominic's eyebrow rose high, "You referring to taking your father's life or is there something else I should know about you, buddy?"

Jessie chuckled humorlessly at Dominic's attempt to lighten the mood, "I've only ever killed twice. Hours after my first shift my father forced my hand when he viciously attacked my mother. Then again earlier today. That's it. But you don't understand. After killing my father, I never recovered. I knew it was a case of either him or my mama leaving that room alive but I still, even now, struggle with the guilt over taking his life. I should have at least tried to find another way.

"I didn't want that dirt to rub off and spoil Kit. She's too good for me, certainly more than I deserve. I was also scared stiff that I would become like my father and start abusing her. Don't worry, Pedro set me straight on that one already, told me I'm more my mother's boy than my father's. He also pointed out that if I was ever stupid enough to raise a hand to Kit, she'd beat my ass into the ground in a heartbeat. I did a lot of thinking on that flight back to Chile. As soon as we took off, Pedro ripped into me, then gave me the silent treatment for the rest of the way."

Dominic chuckled. "Sometimes you need a close friend to point out the obvious. And he's right, Kit wouldn't hesitate, then all her leap brothers would be right behind her for a shot at you. Not to mention you'd have to answer to me and my dad for it as well.

"But I don't get that vibe from you. Trust me, I've seen what makes an abusive asshole tick. Cole, the bastard who hurt Kelly? Now he was, without a doubt, a monster. Months before Kelly escaped, he'd raped and beaten her mother to death. No remorse. Kelly's confided a lot of what she suffered to Adele, who tells me. Within hours of Kelly hearing her mother's final scream, he had Kelly chained up in his basement. Cole had no heart, and he was pure evil. You, my friend, are not anything like that man. You've already shown how deeply you care for Kit. Hell, the second you heard she was in danger you jumped on a plane back here. Sure, leaving in the first place was a mistake, but you came back."

Jessie was stunned mute. He'd never so much as raised a hand to a child, or a woman in his life. He knew to his soul now that he wouldn't. The very idea of what

Dominic described made Jessie's stomach churn uncomfortably.

"What happened to Cole? If you don't mind me asking."

Dominic's grip tightened on the steering wheel until his knuckles turned white. Jessie winced and was about to retract his question when Dominic spoke.

"You're not the only one to make mistakes, Jessie. I made a bad call. I went out when I should have stayed home and Cole took Adele and Kelly. We went to their rescue and I got the pleasure of ripping his throat out. But not before Adele had been forced to fight for her life. She was so damn battered when we got her out. And Kelly, he'd delved into her head and all but destroyed that poor girl."

"Kelly seems like a normal teenager now. How long ago did this all happen?"

"Back in February."

Jessie's jaw went slack with shock. "As in this year? Nine months ago?"

"Yep, that's the one. It's been an eventful year, that's for sure."

Jessie shook his head in amazement. He'd seen Kelly a few times at Kit's place. She was a sweet kid, a little shy around him, but she seemed like any other teen. Of course, he'd never sat down and conversed one-on-one with her, so he couldn't say what she was like personality-wise.

He sighed as Dominic pulled up in front of Kit's

house.

"So, I take it you're definitely here to stay then?"

"I'm not leaving Tasmania. I just hope Kit will let me stay here with her."

"She will. Just be gentle with her and know she feels the same connection you do. She's just being a typical stubborn woman and refusing to give into it. Keep being her rock, and she'll realize you're not going to leave her, and open up. Dad told me not so long ago that Kit's biggest fear has always been rejection from those she cares about, hence her keeping all those secrets. You leaving after the rally cut her to the core."

Jessie's heart cramped in his chest. He'd been so very stupid.

"Yeah, I know. But I'm not going anywhere ever again, at least not without Kit." Jessie looked Dominic in the eye as he shook the man's hand. "Thank you, Dominic. For everything."

"Anytime, Jessie. Oh, and tell Kit she's off the roster for at least the next week at the firehouse. I'll kick her ass if I see her down the station before she's meant to be."

"Oh, she'll love that. I think I'll just tell her to call you. She can rip you apart then, not me."

With a chuckle, Jessie stepped free of the car and headed to Kit's front door as he listened to Dominic make his way back down the road. Jessie thrust his hand into the pocket of his borrowed shorts and sent a silent thank you to Dominic for making him leave his keys and phone in the car before the fight so they didn't get lost when he shifted and tore up his clothes.

Taking a deep breath for calm and patience, he slid his key into the lock and turned it. He silently slipped inside and closed the door as he listened for any sound that would give away Kit's location. He heard nothing but soon spotted her curled up on her couch in her usual position. He made his way over to her, his heart aching more with each step. She was staring out the rear glass doors into the night but didn't look to be actually seeing anything. The tear tracks on her cheeks cut deep into him as he dropped to his knees in front of her. Her hair was damp and he could smell the tang of the organic shampoo she used. She'd put on a clean over-sized shirt and it made her look fragile, even though she was around six feet tall and not a small woman. He cupped her face in his palms and used his thumbs to wipe her tears away before he leaned in to gently brush his lips over hers. When he pulled away, she blinked and focused on his gaze. Her eyes held pain and deep sorrow.

Jessie couldn't think of anything to say. He had no words that would ease her, so he followed his instincts. He rose to stand, lifting her from the seat as he did. She stiffened for a moment, before she relaxed and rested her cheek against his bare shoulder. When she pressed her palm over his heart, his skin tingled beneath her touch. He carried her to her bedroom and lowered her to stand before him. Needing to stay connected to her, he kept a hand on her hip as he leaned around her to pull the covers back on the bed.

"Lay down, *reinita*. You've had a traumatic day and need to rest."

She cocked her head to the side and raised a hand to stroke his face tenderly and the look of fragility in her gaze cracked his heart wide open.

"You came for me."

She thought I wouldn't?

"Of course I returned to you. I would have been here sooner but I went with Dominic for a drive, and I thought you could use a little time to yourself. Kit. You didn't think I'd left you for good, did you?"

Her gaze dropped along with her hand as a light blush colored her cheeks. "Wouldn't be the first time you've run from me."

Her words were like a blade to his heart—and ego. This was his own fault. She'd given him the most precious gift of allowing him to take her virginity and he'd panicked and run off. *Will she ever be able to forgive me?* Dominic's voice played in his mind. *Patience.* He needed patience and kindness, and to think about what he said before he let his temper get the better of him. When they were both fired up, it got intense and they both said shit they shouldn't. Not wanting to cause her any more pain, he didn't say a word as he thought about what his next move should be.

She stood before him wearing nothing but a thin white shirt and she looked so damn breakable and vulnerable. But she wasn't trying to hide from him or push him away. In fact she'd touched him of her own volition twice since he'd walked into her home. Was she softening toward him?

"No more running, I promise. Now, lay down and I'll tuck you in before I go shower, then I intend to sleep beside you."

Her startled gaze shot up to his.

"Don't go worrying, I'm not going to try to get into your pants. I just… Well, I just need to be near you. Hold you and know you're safe. Okay?"

She exhaled on a sigh as she slipped into the bed and allowed him to pull the sheets over her. He leaned down and feathered a kiss over her temple before he headed out of the room toward the bathroom.

Kit fought to find sleep but her brain refused. The moment she'd plunged the blade into Gabriel's chest played over and over in her mind. She knew she hadn't had a choice. If she hadn't killed him, he would have certainly taken her life, so on one hand she felt a level of relief that she no longer had to watch her back waiting for him to find her and attack. But the man was still her father and she could remember how he was with her before everything changed. Family camping trips in the Outback where he taught Kit survival tricks, then over the light of the campfire he would tell her stories and help her roast marshmallows on long sticks she'd found earlier in the day with him by her side.

She growled at herself, her emotions bouncing all over the place after her traumatic day, and she hated it.

She was not an overly emotional person. Ever. Thoughts of her mother crept in. Was her mother still looking for her? Kit chewed her bottom lip as she wondered whether she should head to the mainland and look for Camila.

Soft fingers caressing her face brought her out of her thoughts to focus on Jessie. The other reason her emotions were in a total mess. He completed her while he frustrated the hell out of her. Was he being truthful that he didn't intend to run from her again? Could she risk letting herself fall even deeper for him? She feared he already held her heart, much more and he'd have her soul...then if he abandoned her, what would she have left? How could she go on after his rejection?

"Don't think so hard, *reinita*. Everything will work out, you'll see."

Lost in the tangle of her emotions and thoughts, she hadn't felt Jessie slide into the bed beside her. He pulled her close so he was spooned up behind her with his arm draped over her waist. She wound her fingers between his and brought his hand up close to her face where she laid a kiss on it.

"Were you telling me the truth? About never leaving me again."

He groaned quietly before he firmly kissed the back of her head.

"I don't ever want to be apart from you, Kit. I'll never be able to apologize enough for leaving the way I did, but I promise you I'll never do it again. I've fallen for you, Kit. You have my heart in your palms now and I can't walk away, no matter what happens. I'm just hoping you won't send me away. I don't want to be your shadow, *reinita*, I want to stand at your side as your partner in life. I want to be the one you lean on for strength, the one you turn to for comfort."

Kit swallowed past the lump in her throat. He was saying all these pretty words...

"You watched me murder my father today. You still want me?"

"Oh *reinita*, I'm sure you remember that dream we shared where I told you about my first shift. I was a boy of fifteen when I was forced to take my father's life. Truth be told, that was part of the reason I left you before. I still feel guilty over it. I didn't want to sully your purity with my ugliness. Kit, I've seen how scared you were as a teenager of your father and I saw how he went after you today. It was you or him, just like my father did with me. Gabriel forced your hand. You did what you had to do to keep both yourself and your leap safe. I fully understand that."

"Our leap. Not just mine."

With his lips pressed against her hair, she felt him grin.

"*Si*, our leap. Now, enough talk for one night. Sleep, *reinita*. Tomorrow will come soon enough."

Kit's heart stuttered in her chest. Of all the things she'd anticipated happening tonight, Jessie gently caring for her and admitting his love for her with no expectations was not on the list. Tears sprung to her eyes and she couldn't stop them from falling.

"You're simply too good to be true, Jessie."

Chapter Eleven

Nerves had Jessie's skin feeling overly sensitive and his fingertips were tingling.

"Don't stress, Jessie. We'll find you the perfect ring for Kit."

He had to chuckle at Kelly's enthusiasm.

"It's actually kind of funny. Both Dominic and Conner took Kelly along with Kit to buy jewelry for me and Tina."

Adele wrapped her arm around his and dragged him into the shop where Kelly had disappeared into moments earlier.

"That just proves they're smart. Men simply aren't designed to be able to do this on their own."

Jessie wiped his sweaty palms over his pants. It had been two weeks since that fight and he'd shown every ounce of patience he possessed with Kit. He laid beside her every night, soothed her when she had nightmares and held her when she wept in her sleep. Today was her first day back working and she'd been beyond ready to return. Jessie had learned without a shadow of a doubt that Kit was not the type of woman able to idly sit around, doing nothing.

Kit had been so happy this morning as she'd dressed and eaten the breakfast he'd prepared for her. He'd discovered in the last fortnight how much he enjoyed doing things for Kit. The way she savored every bite of food he prepared for her made him feel like he was ten feet tall, and the way she tenderly stroked his face at night when she thought he was asleep... He sighed at the memory and his heart swelled with love for her.

"Good morning. How can I help you today?"

The perky sales assistant brought him out of his thoughts.

"I need an engagement ring."

Jessie smirked as the young woman all but bounced on the spot.

"Oh, I love helping couples choose their special rings!"

She glanced excitedly over to Adele and her gaze dropped to her left hand. Jessie did his best not to full out laugh at the confounded look on her face. He looked to Adele and saw she was blushing as she realized what the sales assistant had assumed.

"Oh, no! Not me, I'm already married. Kelly and I are just here to help Jessie decide."

Now the sales assistant was blushing more than Adele. Damn women were funny.

"Jessie! Look! It's perfect!"

Kelly had wandered off to look in all the cases and Jessie followed Adele and the sales assistant to her. Under the glass there were dozens of sparkling rings, all different shapes and sizes—and colors.

"Which one do you like, Kelly?"

Before she answered Adele's question, Jessie saw it. The perfect ring for Kit.

"That one there. Third from the left, second row from the back."

He tapped over the glass and the assistant unlocked the case to retrieve the ring. Kelly squealed beside him. "That's the one! Look at it, Adele. Doesn't it just say 'Kit'?"

"I have to agree. It's stunning. Strong lines, simple yet classy."

The young woman behind the counter finally recovered from her earlier embarrassment and rattled off a description of the ring.

"As you can see this beautiful piece has a one point two-five carat, brilliant cut diamond in a semi-bezel end setting. The white gold band has tapered shoulders and inverted sides, which leaves no sharp edges on the ring at all."

"Which is just what I want. Kit rides her motorbike so much, I want her to be able to easily wear this under her gloves."

"This ring will work well for her then. It's all smooth lines so won't catch on her gloves. It's also solid enough that the setting won't be damaged easily. And of course, if she doesn't like it, she can bring it in and we can exchange it for her."

Jessie held the ring in his palm for a moment,

imagining how it would look after he slid it on Kit's finger. His heart picked up speed until it was pounding so loud he could hear it. Would she like it? Or more importantly, would she say yes when he asked her?

"Jessie?"

He glanced to Adele as he wet his dry lips.

"I can see the questions running around your mind. You're the only one who knows whether you're ready to ask her. From what I've seen, she's more than ready to answer."

He took a deep breath and handed the ring back to the shop assistant.

"I'll take it."

Kit felt good. No, she was better than good; she felt fantastic. She'd just stepped free of the shower in the changing room after returning from attending her first fire in weeks. She loved the thrill of racing to the scene and fighting the flames back until they surrendered. She'd never wanted to do anything else with her life. Long ago Jake had explained to her how they were originally created as protectors and that trait carried through to all their kind. She was certainly wired that way, saving lives and property from a fire's hungry mouth was a gratifying experience.

With her shift nearly over, she pulled her bike gear from her locker. After donning her riding pants, she carried her leather jacket, gloves and helmet as she made her way toward the main room where the boys were. She was the only female on team at the station at the moment, but it didn't bother her. There were only a couple of them that weren't her leap brothers, and they didn't mind working with a girl. The few times someone said something to them, they'd just shrugged and said she pulls her weight the same as the men so what does it matter that she's a woman?

Putting her jacket and helmet down on the table, she sat to do up her boots while she chatted with the boys. When she was done, she straightened in her seat and froze when she heard a familiar sound. The loud roar of a Ducati. Holding her breath, she cocked her head to listen more closely.

"That your ride, Kit?"

"Fuck!"

She flew up and sprinted out the side door to the car park. Anyone touching her baby would die. And if someone had stolen it, she'd hunt the bastard down... She stopped in her tracks when she saw her beautiful red Ducati Monster 1100 Evo right where she'd left it this morning. So where was the noise coming from? She walked around to the front of the station in time to see a dark bike pull up. *Oh yeah*. Now that was one fine piece of machinery. She took in all the lines and curves of the bike as she walked closer.

"Ducati Superbike 1198...very nice."

The engine cut out a moment before a deep voice she'd know anywhere filled the air.

"Glad you like it."

She stepped back in shock, "Jessie?"

He pulled his helmet off and Kit nearly drooled watching him swing his long sexy leg over the bike as he dismounted.

"When did you have time to go buy a bike?"

He shrugged a little stiffly, like he was nervous about something.

"I saw it in the shop when I was in Launceston with the rally. Figured since I'm living here now, I should get my own wheels. And really, you've seen the roads on this island, what else would I get? I had to get a bike."

She grinned as she once again looked over the machine behind him.

"I like the red rims and framework."

"Yeah, thought you might. Some local big shot custom ordered it last year but blew his money on a bad investment so couldn't afford to take delivery. Unlucky for him, but very lucky for me. It's perfect and rides like a dream."

He set his helmet on the seat before he unzipped his jacket, revealing a tight shirt that did nothing to hide his ripped his chest and abs. She licked her suddenly dry lips. Jessie prowled over to her and took her face firmly between his palms and kissed her passionately before she could process what was happening. She melted beneath him.

Jessie had been her rock these last two weeks. When she'd raged at him after Dominic had told her she was off roster for a fortnight, he'd just calmly let her get it out of her system before he made her a coffee. He'd sat her down on the couch by his side where he stroked her hair and shoulders after she'd settled down. When she'd woken from her nightmares, it was to find herself securely in his warm embrace. He'd asked for nothing of her the entire time, but gave her everything she'd wanted or needed. If she'd thought she was falling for him before the showdown at the farmhouse, she was now certain she loved this man.

A wolf-whistle behind her had Jessie pulling away from her lips.

"Shut it, Conner."

"Aw, c'mon, man, I'm just paying it forward. They all give me hell whenever Tina drops in."

Kit felt her cheeks heat with embarrassment when she turned to see the whole crew watching. Ignoring them all, Jessie guided her face back to him with a finger under her chin.

"Want to go for a ride with me? Put this baby through its paces?"

She grinned wide as excitement coursed through her.

"Oh, hell yeah! Let me grab the rest of my gear and we can head off."

She spun and strolled back inside as the boys moved in on Jessie and his new toy. Men were so predictable. It would be at least half an hour before they'd be leaving.

Jessie was still chatting to them when Kit slid onto the seat of her bike. She laughed as she turned her Monster over and watched Jessie shoo away the men before getting on his own ride in a rush. She put on and buckled her helmet before she slipped her gloves into place. With the visor up, she rode slowly over to Jessie's side. The sound of the two motors purring together was simply divine. She grinned as she inhaled a deep breath, happiness seeping out of her pores as she took a moment to simply bask in the joy.

"Where did you want to go?"

Jessie shrugged his broad shoulders, "Not sure. Where are some good twisty roads?"

Kit laughed. "This is Tassie! All the damn roads are like that! How about we head down to Zeehan? There's a road that will take us down the edge of the national park to the coast. It has lots of turns too."

Kit laughed as his eyes sparkled with joy. "Yeah, that sounds great. Let's go!"

Jessie felt so alive, his heart racing by the time they pulled up. He cut the Ducati's engine and flipped up his visor. He loved riding, especially when he was on a well-tuned machine. His new baby was perfect. He glanced over to Kit sitting astride her red Ducati as she pulled her helmet free and her red hair cascaded down the back of her black leather jacket. Damn, but she was gorgeous. The fact she adored riding as much as he did was a total bonus. She unzipped her jacket and he nearly swallowed his tongue. She stripped down to a tight singlet top thing. Was that what they called a sports bra? *Who cares?* It looked damn good on her. Even sitting, her stomach was flat and toned with obvious muscle.

"I haven't been out here in ages. When I got my first bike, I'd come down here to this little beach all the time."

Jessie forced his gaze away from the glory of her body and looked around him as he stripped off his gloves. They'd taken a short narrow track down from the road to a low cliff. The hard rock was sturdy under the bike's tires and if they jumped down the foot or so drop, they would be on a white sandy beach. It didn't span far, maybe thirty feet wide. It was like a small piece of paradise, a tiny cove hidden by the surrounding higher rocky cliffs.

"How'd you find it to begin with?"

She looked out over the ocean as she shrugged her shoulders. "Had a lot of time to kill back then and not much to do. I liked exploring."

He watched her closely as he responded, "Yeah, I've always enjoyed my own company. Guess it's our leopards wanting some solace."

Kit didn't answer but turned away from him as she swung her leg over the rear of her bike and dismounted. He wasn't entirely sure what to make of her non-response. With a quiet sigh, he followed her lead and hopped off his bike. He quickly unbuckled his helmet and removed it, taking a deep breath of the fresh air as he unzipped his jacket and shrugged out of it. The day was fairly hot, typical for summer in Australia he was learning. While riding, the wind had kept him cool, but now that he was stationary the sun heated up all the leather he was wearing in no time.

"Damn, it's hot today. Want to take your boots off and go down on the sand?"

Kit's grin was like a ray of sunshine that cut straight to his soul. She was always beautiful but when she smiled like she was now, her whole face lit up and she was beyond gorgeous.

"Sounds good to me."

With her back to him, she peeled her jacket all the way off and Jessie had to remind himself to breathe. Oh yeah, that top was his new favorite. The back was a wide single strap down the center, curling around her shoulder blades before it wound around her ribs. Abandoning the idea of taking off his boots for now, he strode over to Kit and ran his fingers down her spine, before caressing his way around to her tummy. She tensed for a moment before she sighed and leaned back against him. She lifted her arms to wrap her hands around the back of his head. He allowed her to pull him to her and he nuzzled into her neck. Her spicy vanilla scent filled his lungs and his already stiff erection throbbed with need.

Lying beside her every night for the past fortnight and not burying himself deep within her had been hell, but he didn't want to push her. He knew the next time they made love, they would complete the mating...and he wanted Kit to be certain he wasn't going to run off on her again before they took that step. When the time came, he didn't want her tense and caught up with thoughts of his possible rejection. He wanted her soft and willing and entirely in the moment with him. Damn, he hoped she'd say yes.

"You look good enough to eat wearing this little scrap of cloth, *reinita*."

She chuckled and it sounded breathy and so sexy.

"It's what I wear to work every day, Jessie. Nothing special."

"Oh, it's special. It's tight over your flesh and lifts your gorgeous breasts up to stand out proud. Even the way it flows around your shoulder blades turns me on."

She rolled her body against his in a wave of movement and when her firm ass connected with his groin, he hissed. A moment later, she'd turned and he found his mouth on hers, her tongue delving deep to dance with his. He wrapped his arms around her, sliding one hand up her back until her fiery tresses surrounded his fingers. The other hand ran down over her sexy ass and pushed her solidly against him. He caught her moan in his mouth as he took control of the kiss. Her fingers slipped beneath his shirt and ran up his chest, her touch sending sparks through his body. With a gasp, he pulled free of the kiss and looked into her dilated green eyes, and realized that she was everything to him...

In a few quick moves, he released Kit, palmed the ring from his pocket and dropped to one knee. No way was he not going to do this properly.

"I love you, Kit. I vow to you, I will never run from you again, you are my world. Please, say you'll marry me."

He held up the ring and her gaze flicked between it and his face. He watched as her expression changed from arousal to shock, then a wide grin spread over her face and her eyes sheened over with tears as she spoke one whispered word.

"Yes."

Joy ripped through his system like a tornado. With trembling fingers, he took her left hand and slid the ring on before he shot to his feet and gathered her in his arms. Needing an outlet for his excitement, he picked her up and spun her around. She giggled as she gripped his neck. Panting, he lowered her so her feet were back on the ground and took her face between his palms.

"You won't regret it, Kit. I'm going to love you forever, *reinita.*"

"You'd better, Jessie. I love you and I won't accept anything less than forever."

He took her mouth with his and devoured her with his kiss. He loved her sass too.

Dominic was still grinning when he arrived at his parents' home after his shift. He was confident Kit and Jessie's relationship was heading in the right direction.

"You're looking pretty pleased with yourself, son. Care to share?"

"Jessie went and bought a bike. A very nice black Ducati. He rocked up at the end of Kit's shift today to go riding with her."

His dad leaned back in his office chair relaxing at

Dominic's news.

"Did Adele mention what she did today?"

Dominic frowned. "I haven't spoken with Adele since this morning. Why?"

"She and Kelly went shopping with him in town today."

"So?"

"Gee, I don't know, son. What do all you boys take Kelly with you to buy?"

Dominic sucked in a breath. "A ring? Jessie bought an engagement ring for Kit today?"

His father's bright smile gave his answer before he spoke, "Sure did."

"Well, that explains the nervous glint in his gaze this afternoon. I hope she says yes."

"I'm sure she will. I've been keeping an eye on them these last weeks. He's been good to her, patient, kind. He's shown her that he can be relied upon. Kit's a handful at the best of times. Jessie's going to need a boatload of patience to be mated to her."

Dominic chuckled. "Yeah, I love Kit as a sister...but I don't envy Jessie."

"Ah well, there will no doubt come a time you'll eat those words. As their bond strengthens, they are going to be quite the force to be reckoned with."

"Kit already is!"

Jake chuckled. "Well, yes, there is that. Anyway, we have business to discuss. You said you wanted to talk about the Search?"

Pushing aside all other matters, Dominic grew serious and sat down opposite his father.

"I know searching for Lost Ones is important, but I think we need to rethink who we send."

"That's a given. No way will Xander leave now."

"That's not all. Originally we planned to just send three, the twins and Xander."

"Yes, we thought a small group would be more efficient and able to move around without detection."

"I agree, but what if they come across Triggers? With only a couple of them, they'd not stand a chance."

"Okay, I'm listening. What's your idea?"

Dominic took a deep breath to gather strength. His dad was still the alpha. He didn't have to listen to anything Dominic suggested. Jake was perfectly within his rights to make Dominic wait until he was alpha himself, but Dominic knew his dad, and he was fairly certain Jake would go for his idea.

"A larger team. Half focused on Lost Ones, half on Trigger and keeping them all protected."

Jake frowned at him for a moment. "How many are you talking?"

"Well, the group we had at the farmhouse worked well. That was fourteen, but I don't think we need that many. Maybe six to ten? We need to keep the number even and paired up, so no matter what happens everyone has someone at their back."

Dominic was grateful his dad was listening. He'd been thinking this through for a while.

"Who are you thinking of?"

"I'd like Xander to head it up. We'd be stupid to not have Kit involved, so Jessie goes too. That boy is already good in a fight. I don't doubt Kit will begin working with him on increasing his skills as soon as things settle down for them. Not to mention he can drive just about anything. The twins are both tech savvy. We're going to need good computer skills on the team. Bently showed his usefulness at the farmhouse. He's clever and doesn't get intimidated. He'll ferret out any information he can with no fear, and he'll never back down unless he has to. That gives us six. To test how they work together, I want to send them down to Hobart. Let them, as a unit, investigate Classic Convicts."

Jake was silent a moment, and Dominic watched nervously as Jake squinted and rubbed his jaw in thought.

"I like how you're thinking, except I'm not sure Xander will have his head in the game for this. His mate is in that building—and engaged to another man."

"I've thought of that too. I think it would be good for you to join the team this first time. Just in an advisory role. That way, not only will you be on hand to advise them, but you can monitor them, see how they function together."

"The idea has possibilities. But the biggest hurdle is losing that many firefighters in one hit. Especially in the middle of fire season. I assume you want to get this off the ground soon?"

Little did Jake know, Dominic had that all sorted. He grinned broadly at his father. "Ye of little faith!"

Jake chuckled. "You are looking like the cat that caught the canary. What did you do, son?"

"I spoke with Ryder this afternoon."

"And what did the good captain of the Hobart Firehouse have to say?"

"That he likes the idea of an exchange, starting after the New Year. There's five good strong firies on the team, Ryder is more than happy to send five of his guys to us. You know our station has a reputation all over the state for being one of the best functioning crews. We're going to do team building stuff with the visitors, show them how much easier it is when everyone plays nice with each other."

His father was nodding as his smile grew wider. "Hmmm. The more I think about this, the better it sounds. If we can get a well-functioning team working, they can travel all over the globe, especially with Jessie rallying. We can easily use that to move the team in to those areas."

Pride bloomed in Dominic's chest at the fact his father liked and supported his concept. Dominic took his role as future alpha seriously and already had a number of ideas that he was working on that would better the leap. He was extremely grateful his dad was open to hearing him out and willing to implement them. So many future alphas had to sit on their grand plans until they had the top job.

"Okay, Dominic, this is your idea so I'm going to let you talk to the guys you want on that team. Let me know when you need help, but this is your baby. And, son, I'm so damn proud of you. You're going to make an excellent alpha one day."

Chapter Twelve

Kit whooped in joy as she powered out of a corner. She knew she was grinning like a fool but she didn't care, and with her helmet on, no one could see it anyhow. Jessie had proposed. He'd been her shadow these past two weeks, and despite her telling Jessie she didn't, it turned out she'd needed one. But it was the nights that were starting to get her worried. She could see and feel how aroused he was each night when he climbed into bed with her but he'd simply hold her and soothe her to sleep. She'd begun to wonder if he was scared to have sex with her. Then again, considering what happened after their first attempt, she had to admit she was hesitant about it herself.

Kit lifted her left hand from the grip and flexed her fingers, feeling the still slightly odd sensation of having a ring on her third finger. She loved it. The piece was simple yet classy, and it had smooth lines that allowed her to wear it with her gloves. It just proved once more how well Jessie had gotten to know her. He'd told her he was careful to select something that she would be able to wear while riding. And the rock in it wasn't bad either! She'd never really taken much notice of diamonds

before, but the way this one sparkled in the sunlight...
She sighed.

Reaching her home, she pulled into her driveway and
flipped her visor up to watch Jessie roll in on his ride.
Damn, but the man looked good on a bike. She sat
transfixed as he swung his lean leg over the rear of his
Ducati and pulled his helmet free. He glanced over at her
with a raised eyebrow along with a cheeky smirk, which
snapped her out of her stupor and she got with the
program. Within moments she was off her bike and
unlocking her front door. She shrugged out of her jacket
and hung it on the hook in the foyer. Her gloves went on
the side table, along with her helmet. The light glinted off
her new ring and she stilled to examine it. It was
beautiful. A solid thick band of white gold surrounding
one hell of a rock, and it had slid free of her glove
without catching on anything. *Perfect*.

She felt Jessie's body heat on her back a moment
before she felt his hands caress their way over her hips.
When she felt his breath on her ear, she tilted her head to
give him room. Nosing her hair out of his way, he
nuzzled against her throat with a purr. Goosebumps rose
on her skin as he feathered kisses up her neck.

"Do you like your ring, *reinita*?"

"I love it. It's perfect. When did you have time to get
it?"

He'd bought her ring and his bike without her having
even a hint of what he'd planned. She was curious how
he'd managed it.

"I had a busy day today. Adele and Kelly went with me to the jewelers. Kelly and I spotted that one at the same time and we both knew it was meant to be yours. Adele agreed. Then they were kind enough to drive me into Launceston so I could pick up my bike. As I said, I'd seen it in their window during the rally so had rung ahead, and they had all the paperwork ready to go."

One of Jessie's hands left her waist and headed north. His fingers flirted with the bottom edge of her sports bra as he continued to lay kisses over her jaw and cheek. She leaned back against him, wrapping an arm around his head to hold him close. He felt so strong and solid against her and she loved it. Her skin was tingling all over as he brought up his other hand and peeled her top off over her head. The world spun and she squealed a little when her spine met the cold plaster of the wall. She arched away from the coolness and with a growl, Jessie took a nipple into his mouth as he ran a hand up between her shoulder blades to hold her against his mouth. Her mind went a little fuzzy as arousal coursed through her. She wove both hands into his thick hair, running her fingers through the silky strands before stroking his broad shoulders through his shirt. She fisted her hands into each side of the material and tugged it up, needing to feel his skin against hers.

Taking the hint, Jessie took a step back and tore his shirt from his body. When his chest was revealed, every ounce of moisture in Kit's mouth vanished. He was magnificent. Broad shoulders, biceps roped with muscle.

His defined pectorals were hair free and gorgeous. His abs were stunning. She could clearly see his six pack, along with the trail of hair that started below his belly button and disappeared into his pants. She licked her lips as she allowed her gaze to lower to the bulge of his erection.

A groan filling the air gave her a moment's warning before Jessie let loose on her. He tore into the front closure of her pants, and dropping to his knees before her, he wrenched them down her legs, taking her panties with them. She still had her boots on but apparently Jessie didn't have the patience to remove them. He pulled her ankles as far apart as they could go within the confines of the material surrounding them as he buried his face between her thighs.

She slapped her palms against the wall as her body shuddered. He suckled her clit as he slowly thrust a finger into her channel. Heat bloomed throughout her body before settling low in her belly as she opened her mouth to take in more air. His finger slid free and she growled at the emptiness she felt. Jessie purred as he ran his tongue over her folds. She jerked against the wall as he tormented sensitive nerves. When he pushed two fingers into her tight sex, she cried out and banged her head against the wall. She clenched her internal muscles as he teased her clit with his tongue, then she began to ride his hand. When he sucked hard on her clit at the same time he thrust into her, she shot over the edge and came.

"Jessie!"

With her screams in his ears, Jessie pulled his fingers free of her clenching channel and reached under her ass to grip her. He slid her down the wall a fraction as he shouldered her knees wider. He covered her core with his mouth as he lapped up every ounce of cream she'd given him. She tasted so damn sweet and he'd never get enough of her. He purred as he realized she was going to be his forever. Every morning he could wake her up like this, and have his fill of her.

Kit shivered in his grip and moaned as she squirmed against the wall. His dick was iron hard and pressing against his zipper like it could break free on its own. He gave her one final lick and she jerked against him. With a grin of deep satisfaction, he pressed a kiss to her lower belly before he set about removing her boots and pants. Once naked, he looked up to her from his position on the floor and his heart stopped a moment, before speeding up to double time.

She was glorious. Her chest heaved with her breaths, making the tight little dark pink nipples that topped her firm delicious breasts rise and fall in the most enticing manner. Her arms and torso were female perfection. Kit was fit, toned and muscled in just the right way. She still had curves. Oh hell, did she have curves. Her hips flared out in a way that made his breath catch every time he saw her. And her ass... Even when she was storming away from him in a rage, the way her ass swayed got him as hard as granite.

There was something extra special about her in this moment, though. The way she looked standing above him covered in sweat and flushed from the orgasm he'd given her...it touched him soul deep. His dick throbbed with his need to be inside her and he refocused his attention. In a heartbeat, he shot up to his feet and gathered her in his arms before he raced towards the bedroom. She reached up and stroked his face as he strode down the hall. Her tender touch seared him. Once in the bedroom, he lightly tossed her onto the mattress so he could tear himself free of his own pants and boots. He was desperate to be naked with her.

"I need to have you, Kit. I can't wait any longer."

Once he was finally free of all his clothing, he climbed on the mattress and prowled over to her. As he closed in on her, she spread her thighs and gifted him with a view of her glistening sex, which beckoned to him. Lowering down, unable to ignore her musky scent, he swiped his tongue over her core just once as he moved up her body. He stopped again for a moment or two to suckle her nipples. They were irresistible, as they stood up for him in tight little peaks, begging for his touch. As he sucked and lapped at her breasts, Kit's lithe body undulated beneath him. He hissed as she pressed her slick heat against the head of his erection.

"That feels so damn good, *reinita*."

Holding himself up on his arms, he watched her as he tilted his pelvis and slid deep within her body. He loved how her face flushed and her eyes dilated. She wrapped her hands around the back of his neck and held on as she moved with him. Like two puzzle pieces, they fit together perfectly. With Kit's heat engulfing his erection and her slender fingers sliding through his hair, Jessie's mind whirled into overdrive.

Jessie had been with a lot of women, and had sex in all sorts of places and ways—but nothing had ever felt as good as sheathing himself inside Kit. She was soft and sweet, yet tough and more than strong enough to handle all of him. Damn, if he'd just known what his dreams of her had meant, he'd have come looking for her long ago. Had this paradise sooner...

"You okay, Jessie?"

He closed his eyes for a moment as he mentally shook himself. He was balls deep in the woman he loved and he was getting caught up in his head. *Idiot*. He looked into her gaze and winced. Her eyes clearly showed her fear. She was on the verge of panicking, no doubt thinking he was about to reject her. Dominic had warned him how she feared it, and he'd already dished it out once to her when he'd run off after the first time they'd had sex. This now, with what he was feeling for her, it was more than sex. So very much more. Shifting his weight to one arm, he raised the other hand to caress her face.

"I love you, Kit. Mate with me. Wear my mark so the world knows you're mine. Mark me so the world knows that somehow, even though I'm a stupid fool who keeps mucking up, you still claim me as your one and only."

Every muscle in Jessie's body went tense as Kit's eyes filled with tears. Had he misread her feelings for him? Did she only want to get married, not mated? He wasn't sure what would change between them by completing the mating, but he knew he wanted everything with Kit. He wanted to find every way he could to bind her to him. He never wanted to be apart from her.

"Please, *reinita*, end my misery and answer me. Your tears are breaking my heart."

In one swift move he barely saw coming, she hooked her leg around his and rolled them over so she straddled him, his dick still hard inside of her, twitching at her show of strength. With a moan, he buried his fingers into her thick red tresses as she lowered her face to his. She took his mouth and proceeded to kiss him until his mind whirled and arousal had his entire being pulsing with heat. He groaned as she swiveled her pelvis against his and he felt the rush of cream that left her core. Kit was killing him. Wrapping her hair around his fists he gently tugged her a little from his lips.

"Is that a yes?"

"Yes, Jessie. Most definitely yes. I love you. I thought," she paused to swallow. "I thought you were going to leave just now. When you stopped and frowned-"

"I'm sorry, *reinita*. I was just kicking myself for wasting so many years. If I'd just known you were real, I could have found you sooner..."

"I'm sorry too, Jessie. I've said things to you that were

harsh and cruel. I wouldn't have blamed you if you had left me."

He released her hair and cupped her face in his hands, the red waves falling around them like a curtain and the floral scent of her shampoo filled the air.

"Look into my eyes, Kit. I will never leave you again. What will it take for you to believe me? I've been trying to do as you asked, to be by your side, not become your shadow."

Her eyes filled with tears once more as a small smile flittered over her face.

"You are so much more than a shadow that follows me around, Jessie. You're my rock. With all the shit I've been throwing around this last fortnight, you stayed through it all, solid and strong. You've more than proved you're not going to leave. But, Jessie? No matter how I present myself to the outside world, I have insecurities that will never go away. Jake's forever telling me I worry too much about being left behind by people who will never reject me, but I can't help it. I'm kind of high maintenance that way. Can you live with that?"

He grinned at how cute she looked perched above him, putting her heart out there for him. He pulled her down to him so he could kiss her with all the love he had for her.

"So long as it means I get you forever, I can live with any and all of your quirks, Kit."

Warmth spread from her chest and throughout her

body until her fingers and toes tingled with it. Jessie continued to melt her heart with each word he spoke. She adored him for his easy acceptance of her quirks. She caressed her fingers over his chest and down his torso as she rose to sit up. Gripping his ribs, she began moving against him.

As she rose and fell she could feel him hardening and lengthening inside of her. She moaned in bliss as he once more filled her completely. His hands rose to torment her breasts, he tweaked and rolled her nipples and she threw her head back on a gasp as strings of pleasure raced from where he tugged at her to join the ever tightening coil of need in her lower belly. He raised his hips as she rode him and Kit relished the way he felt beneath her. She instinctively knew he wouldn't allow her control of their night for long so she intended to make the most of it. The next time he seated himself fully, she twisted her hips in a circle over him and purred when she felt him tense beneath her with a groan.

As she slid her hips against him, and his hands continued to play and torment her breasts, she raised her arms and folded them behind her head as she arched her back pushing her chest toward him. She felt so alive, every nerve was buzzing and ready to explode. With a growl, he sat up and curled an arm around her back to hold her still as he lifted a breast to his mouth with his other hand. She jerked in his embrace as he sucked hard at the same time he thrust up into her. She lowered her arms and dug her fingers into his shoulders as desire and arousal built even higher inside of her.

"Jessie..."

His name was a plea, one that he answered. She shocked herself by whimpering when Jessie lifted her from his erection. Before she could say anything, he had her flipped onto all fours and was guiding his thick length back into her core. She moaned as he scraped over sensitive nerves and she pushed against him when he began to withdraw once more. Kit wanted him deep, so far inside her they would meld into one. He leaned over and kissed her shoulder.

"I love you, *reinita*."

As he whispered to her, he gripped his fingers around her hips and began pounding into her and took away all her ability to think. She moved with him, relishing how the coil in her lower belly kept tightening with each stroke. His movements sped up at the same moment she felt his fingers on her clit. It felt like she'd been struck by lightning and she jerked while he toyed with her. His thrusts built in speed and she knew he was as close to coming as she was. Her whole body jolted when he took a mouthful of her flesh at the join of her neck and shoulder. His possessive hold of her, the strong powerful strokes of his thick erection inside of her and his clever fingers on her clit—were all more than she could stand and she thrashed beneath him as her world blew apart with enough force she saw stars. As she went flying, she felt him twitch within her and heard his low growl as he joined her.

"Kit, help me. What do I do? My claws... I don't want to hurt you."

He licked over her neck, where he'd bitten her and she shuddered as aftershocks plowed through her body. After taking a deep breath for strength, she put her weight on one arm as she reached down with her right hand to take his palm in hers. She placed it over her right hipbone.

"Press your claws into my skin, then drag them back. It's magic based, it's not really going to cut into me."

Her words were raspy and hoarse and she hoped he'd been able to hear her. Tears pricked her eyes as his lips pressed against her shoulder blade and she felt the heat and spark of the mark appearing as he dragged his claws over her flesh. Her own hand began to tingle as her claws sprouted. She moved forward to dislodge his penis from her and rolled onto her back. She cupped his face with her left hand while she pressed her right over his heart and digging her claws in, she dragged downward in an arc over his heart. He shuddered and gasped while she watched in awe as her mark appeared on him.

Kit didn't even try to stop the tears. She was ecstatically happy. Something shifted within her soul and she knew Jessie would now be inside of her forever. She was finally whole and complete. Once her claws disappeared, she pressed her palm over the four scratch marks that revealed leopard spots on his chest, purring when tingles ran up her arm.

"Put your palm over your mark on me, Jessie. Feel the magic."

Jessie rolled to the side a little and reached over to cover her hip. He jolted on a gasp before his eyes grew wet with unshed tears.

"Wow."

Kit smiled up to him as she pulled him down to her for a kiss without removing her palm from his chest. He came to her without restraint, eating at her mouth like he'd never tasted anything better. As her body heated up for him again, she wound both hands into his hair and rolled over to land on top of him. His palms moved to grip her hips and help her glide down his once more lengthening erection as he filled her again.

"Hmmm," she hummed as she straightened her spine, and began to ride him slow and easy. The connection felt so much stronger now they were mated. Jessie cupped her hips and took control of her movements. She lowered so her breasts were pressed against his hard chest and she could kiss his gorgeous mouth again. With a purr, Jessie rolled them over so he was on top. He lifted one of her legs up high over his hip as he ground against her. Her eyes flew wide as he hit new nerves deep within her.

"Like that, *reinita*?"

"Hmmm."

She couldn't form words with him taking her breath away like he was. A hum of approval was all she was capable of. He didn't seem to mind as with a chuckle he lowered his lips to devour her mouth as he blew apart her world once more and left his mark on not only her skin, but her heart and soul as well.

Chapter Thirteen

Xander rolled his shoulders as he pulled up into Top Pub's car park. He didn't want to be here. He was tired and on edge, which put him in a foul mood. He'd been spending as much time as he could in Hobart, trying to get close to his mate, but being mid-December, it was smack bang in the middle of fire season, so he couldn't take time off from work. As much as he'd been relieved to see Rachel worked the bar at HoHaven, not the poles, he still couldn't stand her being there. Xander would never make his mate work in such a place. He certainly wouldn't maul her in public like that bastard did.

With a growl, he slammed his door as he thought about how Rocco paraded her around. He may as well put her up on the stage wrapped around a pole. Rachel's expression clearly showed how uncomfortable she was with the attention. She might wear the guy's ring, but she didn't seem real fond of him. But Rocco was Trigger. If he caught Xander sniffing around, and worked out what he was, he'd know who Rachael was to him and Xander held no illusions as to how Rocco would treat Rachel then. If only Trigger weren't involved, he could start romancing her away from Rocco and into his arms where she belonged. As much as he knew kidnapping her was out of the question—and illegal—he was sorely tempted to simply snatch her and take her home with him.

Xander stretched out his neck as he stalked away from his car. He couldn't keep going with what he was doing, which was basically stalking her whenever he wasn't on shift. He'd learned a lot about her habits and those of the owner and staff of Classic Convicts, but he'd barely slept in the past month and the fatigue was beginning to show and effect his thought processes. He'd also noticed his reflexes were becoming slower each day. He knew something had to give.

"Hey, Xander."

Xander jerked his head up at the sound of Dominic's deep voice to see that he'd managed to walk all the way to Top Pub's back room without being aware of it. Damn, he really needed a decent night's sleep. He couldn't afford to ignore his surroundings like this. Especially with the potential threat of Trigger so close.

"Hey, Dom. What's this all about?"

"Let's just wait for the others. Then I'll explain it all."

"If this is about the Search, I can't go anymore. You know why. I'm not going anywhere until I have Rachel safe and claimed."

Even before finding Rachel, he'd been hesitant to go on the Search. The mess his father had made of things by going looking for his mate had been the only reason Xander hadn't already gone off on his own search. While his father had been scouring the mainland for Beverley, she'd moved to Tasmania for work. They'd wasted so much time running around in circles. A year or so after he'd started dreaming of his British accented beauty, Xander had sat down with Choden to discuss mates. Choden confirmed the theory that eventually fate always made paths cross for mates. Choden had told him when he was ready, his female would come to him here in Tasmania. Somehow the ancient monk had known his mate wasn't Australian, without him having to say a word.

Dominic rubbed his jaw as he looked Xander in the eye.

"It is about the Search, but I'm pretty sure you'll like what I have to offer, so sit down—before you fall over—and wait for the others."

Xander did his best not to growl at his captain and future alpha as he all but collapsed into a chair. Shit, he was wiped out.

"Before the others get here, I will say this. You need to manage your time better. You need sleep. It's not negotiable. If you refuse to look after yourself, what I'm about to put on the table will never work."

He frowned as he looked up at Dominic. What the hell was he talking about? Before he could ask anything else the others came in. Kit and Jessie came in holding hands looking way too happy. As Kit walked, he caught a flash of her hip between her low riding jeans and tight black tee. It had four scratch marks that hadn't been there before. Fuck, they'd completed the mating. As happy as he was for them, he couldn't help but rub over the ache in his chest as an image of Rachel flashed into his mind. When the hell would he get his shot at forever? He'd been dreaming of her for four long years, and now that their paths had finally crossed, she was claimed by a member of their enemy.

"Xander?"

Shaking his head to clear his mind, he glanced up to see that Jordan, Joel and Sean had entered the room.

"Sorry, just lost in thought."

"You right to do this now? Or do I need to send you home to sleep for the night and we'll meet again tomorrow?"

Xander curled his lip in anger and embarrassment. "I'm perfectly fine, Dominic. Quit wasting time and get on with it."

Dominic crossed his arms over his muscled chest and stared at him. Xander couldn't take it and jerked up out of his seat and crossed over to where there was a tea and coffee station set up. It was only instant crap but it had caffeine so it would do the job. He made himself a strong coffee—no milk or sugar—before he returned to his seat.

"Okay, so I have a proposition for you all. I ran it past dad and as alpha he's keen for me to go ahead with it so I called you all here."

Xander leaned back and stretched his legs out before Dominic continued. Thankfully the coffee was working and he was feeling more alert now. He had a feeling he didn't want to miss any of what Dominic was about to say.

Kit stayed silent as she glanced around the room when Dominic finished his spiel, gauging the reactions of the men.

"So, to break it down, you want the six of us to form a team that goes out and deals with Trigger while searching for lost ones?"

"Yes, Xander. That's what I'm saying. I want you to train together to become a tight functioning group. We wiped out the cell of Triggers here locally, but that club down in Hobart is a bigger base for them. We need to shut that down, and rescue Rachel along with any other innocents. For this first assignment dad will go with you, help advise you and pick up any slack."

Kit stood away from the wall she'd been leaning against. "Why us? I understand Xander's involvement. Rachel is his mate. But why the six of us in particular?"

"Because of your skills. Rachel aside, I still wanted Xander in on this. Xander is a strong leader, and when he's not sleep deprived from chasing his mate down, he has a clear head and makes good decisions quickly. He will be the alpha of the team. Joel and Jordan are tech. They can build, create, destroy, and hack into anything electronic. Sean, he's the negotiator. He's like a dog after a bone when on a mission and he will never back down. He'll also find a person's weakness in a heartbeat. Jessie, your driving skills will come in very handy, as will your knowledge of so many different places. We'll also use your rallying as a reason to globe trot. You, Kit, you're our fighting expert. You can kick anyone's ass, but you're going to need to share your skills, sister. I want you to train the team so they can all fight at a higher level than they currently do."

Kit paced across the room and back as the boys all put in their willingness to form the team. Everyone had agreed...except her.

"Kit? You in?"

She frowned over at Dominic. "I've got some conditions. First off, I don't have an issue training anyone. No matter what happens, I'll do that. But after we do this thing in Hobart, I need to find my mother." She held her hand up to stop Dominic talking when he tried to cut her off. "Gabriel told me she left him six months after they kicked me out. She didn't agree with what happened and wanted to find me. He said he only kept tabs of her movements for a while, he couldn't—or wouldn't—tell me where she is currently."

"So what you're asking is that we add your mother on to the list of lost ones? Near the top?"

"The very top. Yes. If the team helps me find my mother, I'm in."

With his hands on his hips, Dominic gave her a sharp nod.

"Done. Give the twins all the information you have on her and she'll go into the list they're going to start investigating."

"Shall do. Thanks."

Relief poured through her as she allowed Jessie to wrap his arms around her waist and pull her back against his chest. She hadn't been sure the boys would agree. It wasn't the best use of this new team but Kit couldn't leave it alone. Ever since Gabriel mentioned it, it had weighed on her mind. She needed to find her mother and reconnect, if she could. If she turned out to be as crazy as the old man? Well, she'd have the team right there by her side to deal with it.

"I've got a couple of questions, Dom. How much of the year will we be traveling? Our families aren't going to like us permanently gone; neither are our mates as we find them."

Dominic turned toward Sean with his hands on his hips.

"We'll start the Hobart gig after New Year's, and I've arranged with the firehouse down there to do an exchange of teams. But after that, I was thinking you would go out for the six months over winter, then be here for the fire season. If you're needed during summer again, we'll need to arrange team exchanges to keep the town covered. It seems we have quite the reputation for being a well-functioning firehouse, so other stations are jumping at the chance to learn from us. It shouldn't be too hard to work out. What else did you want to ask, Sean?"

"We going to get paid for this? Not that I wouldn't love to do it anyway, but eating and having a roof over my head are things I'd like to keep."

Kit chuckled with the others at Sean's attempt to

lighten the question, but he raised a good point. While they earned enough to live on firefighting, it hadn't made any of them rich enough to be able to afford to not work for half of every year.

"Dad spoke with Choden earlier today. He said he'd make sure we were adequately funded. Before you ask, I don't know. Choden has always kept himself a mystery from everyone, so I don't know how much money he has, or what his definition of 'adequately funded' is exactly."

Xander shifting to sit forward in his chair had the room silent in seconds.

"You honestly think I'm going to wait two weeks to see Rachel again?"

Kit leaned back against Jessie, absorbing his warmth. Xander radiated cold fury as he stared Dominic down. The shadows under his eyes showed how sleep deprived the bloke was. Kit wouldn't ever want to be on the wrong side of Xander, and as tired and on edge as he was, she didn't think it would take much at the moment to end up there.

"No, Xander, I would never expect any shifter to abandon his mate once he found her. From now until we officially start, we'll rotate surveillance. But that is all that will be done. No contact, unless of course she is in immediate danger. If that happens, whoever is on duty will call in the team and we'll take it from there. Understand? I'm serious about you looking after yourself, Xander. You need to sleep, or you'll be useless."

Xander didn't look happy as he crossed his arms across his chest, but he didn't argue.

"Anything else you want to ask, Sean?"

"Just one more question. What happens when we claim our mates?"

"Hopefully they'll form part of the team. If they want to join, we'll find them a role. If not, and you decide to leave, we'll work around it. I'm not asking for lifetime oaths here, guys. There are always options on how to move forward. I don't want any of you doing this if you truly don't want to. Now, anyone else have an issue with starting in the new year?"

"I would like to be married to Kit before we start this endeavor."

Dominic turned his attention to Jessie as Kit stiffened against him. Jessie would have liked to have discussed this with Kit alone before including anyone else, but that option wasn't really available to him.

"Not sure that's going to work Jessie. Here in Tasmania you need to lodge a notice with the authorities a month before you intend to get married. We can't put this off that long, not with Xander's mate in the middle of things."

Jessie started to turn over a few ideas when Kit turned to look up at him.

"It's not the end of the world if we get married while we're working. Neither of us have huge families to invite. We could do something low-key like down on the beach or something. We can honeymoon after we finish up in Hobart."

He pressed a quick kiss to her lips before returning his attention to Dominic.

"Okay, we'll work something out. We're in."

A grin spread over Dominic's face.

"Great! I can't thank you all enough for this. I'm hoping other leaps will follow our lead and create similar teams but potentially you guys could be sent all over the globe on missions. You'll all need to train and up your skills."

Jessie had no issue with that, he'd committed to living a lifestyle based on traveling internationally when he signed up with his current rally team. So long as he was with Kit, it didn't bother him where they lived.

"How soon do you want me to start training with everyone? It would be good to have at least started before we left for Hobart."

"I agree, Kit. How about you draw up a plan today and we'll meet again tomorrow to nail out the finer details. I've found a house to rent that will easily accommodate you all. It's located about ten minutes from both the Classic Convicts and the firehouse. It doesn't have much of a backyard, so when you need to go for a run, you'll need to head out of town. I tried to find something that backed onto bushland but there was nothing close to where you need to be."

After they all agreed to meet back here the next evening, Jessie took Kit's hand and headed out of the pub. He needed to spend some time on the internet and make a few calls.

"You're quiet, Jessie. What are you thinking?"

He smiled down at Kit. He hadn't meant to worry her. "I'm trying to think of a way to marry you before we go to Hobart. I may have an idea but need to look into it a little before I get either of our hopes up."

She wrapped her arm around his as they made their way toward her house. Top Pub wasn't far so they'd decided against riding so they could stay close to each other as they walked.

"Well, it's going to take me some time to put together training sessions and I don't need my computer to do it, so help yourself and see what you can find. I would rather get married before we start, but like I said, I don't mind waiting. We're mated and that's forever."

"I haven't had as long as you to get used to all the shifter stuff. I need to marry you to make it feel real to me. I also want you to take my name."

"There's my caveman. You just want to brand me with your name as well as your mark."

He chuckled. Of course he wanted to mark her in every way possible, but it wasn't only that.

"I love you, Kit, and I don't care if it makes me a caveman. I want you to not only have my mark on your skin, but wearing my ring on your finger and changing your last name to mine. As soon as possible."

Kit pulled him to a stop on the side of the road and dragged his face to hers for a heat filled kiss.

"I love you, and of course we'll get married. I wasn't saying I didn't want to. As a shifter, I believe that the mating is the true bonding of two people forever. Marriage is still an important part..." She paused on a sigh. "I'm not explaining this well. I guess I'm trying to say, in my mind the mating was us getting married."

He smiled down at her. She really was cute when she got flustered.

"You know, I liked the idea you mentioned earlier and was thinking along the lines of a beach ceremony. In Chile. But I really do need to take a look at the internet and check a few things out."

Kit's eyes widened. "Chile?"

"Yes, Kit. We're both Chilean by birth. It will probably be easier for us to marry there. But I have no idea about how long you need to register the paperwork before you can get married. Give me some time. I'll sort something out. You focus on training our leap brothers to be a bunch of martial arts experts. Leave the wedding to me."

She laughed as he'd wanted her to.

"I think we've reversed roles here. It's meant to be the girl that does all the wedding stuff."

"Ah well, since when have we done anything the right way around?"

"There is that. Oh, just remember Conner and Tina are getting married Christmas day so we need to be here for that."

"I'm sure we can work around it, *reinita*."

As Kit unlocked the house, Jessie couldn't wait to get to work. The sooner he worked out how long they needed to be in Chile to file the paper work and get married, the sooner he could plan it all and have Kit tied to him in every way he knew of.

Chapter Fourteen

"C'mon, Aunty Kit! Get out of bed already."

Kit opened one eye to watch Kelly dance around the room excitedly.

"How'd you get in here, kiddo?"

She stopped and grinned broadly. "Uncle Jessie loaned me his key."

Kit snorted a little as she buried her face back in her pillow. She doubted Jessie simply offered Kelly the keycard. More likely, Kelly either charmed him to hand it over or stole it from his pocket. The kid was sneaky.

She jerked and gripped the covers when she felt them move down her body.

"Kelly! Stop! I'll get up. I've got nothing on under these sheets! You can't just rip them off me."

"Oh. Um. Okay. I'll just face the wall here while you make yourself decent then."

Kit rubbed her face as she sat up, before she yanked the top sheet off the bed to wrap it around her body.

"Okay. I'm decent. You know, it's my wedding day. I should be able to sleep in."

Kelly turned on her with folded arms and a serious expression. She looked so cute trying to be all stern and mature, Kit started laughing.

"Don't you laugh at me! This is my third wedding in the last six months. Trust me, the bride never gets to sleep in. Except you apparently. It's already nine o'clock. That is a sleep in."

With a gasp of shock, Kit glanced at the clock to confirm Kelly wasn't exaggerating.

"Okay, didn't realize it was that late. Let me shower and we'll get moving."

Kelly moved over to the small table near the window and pulled free a sheet of paper from her pocket.

"What's that, Kelly?"

Kit rose and went to her bag to gather her underwear before she snatched up the robe the hotel had provided her with, for her morning appointments.

"Today's schedule. I'm your only *Madrina de Matrimonia*, and I take the role seriously."

Kit tilted her head. "Who taught you that phrase?"

Kelly winced as she blushed. "I said it wrong, didn't I? Pedro had me chanting it last night until I got it right. I was sure I'd nailed it."

"You said it perfectly, Kelly. I was just curious who'd taught you how to say bridesmaid in Spanish."

"Well, now you know, and you only have half an hour before we need to be out that door. Quit talking, and start showering."

Kit shook her head on another laugh.

"Pushy little thing aren't you, kiddo?"

"Sure am. Just you remember it, and today will run

smoothly."

Still chuckling, Kit shut the door and turned on the shower as she listened to Kelly mutter about already running late before the first appointment.

Jessie had continued to do everything completely backward, but it totally worked for them. After searching the internet, Jessie discovered it was only an eight day wait in Chile and in that time the couple needed to do a course. So they'd decided to have their honeymoon first, then get married.

On the twenty-seventh of December, two days after Conner and Tina tied the knot, she and Jessie had flown to Arica, Chile. Pedro had greeted them at the airport and brought them to a glorious hotel situated on the coast, surrounded by beaches on three sides. For the past eight days, Jessie had treated Kit like a princess and shown her around Arica. She'd seen the house he grew up in. The one he and his mother shared with others after his first shift. He'd even taken her for a drive to show her where he'd first driven a rally car. Yesterday he'd taken her to meet his mother. Kit's heart broke a little as she watched Jessie dissolve before her tombstone. It was clear Jessie loved his mother deeply, and still felt her loss close to his heart.

She'd barely lifted a finger all week. Jessie had taken care of everything. The only thing he'd left to her was the dress. He'd dropped her off at a boutique in Arica and she'd found the perfect gown hanging on the rack. It fit her like a glove, as if it had been waiting for her to come and claim it.

Kit wasn't normally comfortable with having such little control, but she only spoke basic Spanish and she trusted Jessie, so she had simply sat back and enjoyed her holiday. And her man. She sighed. Jessie loved her so well and often, she tingled between her thighs all the time. It was a good feeling. Her heart was full, her mind at ease, and her body fully relaxed.

Then last night, Jessie had taken her out for dinner. Which wasn't unusual, but the fact that the restaurant contained Choden, Jake, Sophie, Dominic, Adele, Kelly and Pedro, along with the local alpha Fernando and his wife Claudia, wasn't the norm. The whole night had been wonderful. There had been great Chilean food and fantastic company to complete the evening. Then back at the hotel, Jessie grabbed his bag, kissed her goodnight and left her alone. According to her mate and fiancé, they'd messed with enough traditions and shouldn't tempt fate by ignoring any more. It was in the rules that the groom couldn't see the bride on their wedding day before the ceremony, so that's how it was going to be.

It had taken Kit hours to settle down to sleep. She'd become accustomed to sleeping next to Jessie, having his body heat keep her warm while his strong arms kept her safe and protected through each night.

Stepping free from the shower, she forced her mind back to current matters. She had a morning of appointments to primp and beautify every inch of her. She hoped she didn't end up losing her mind and lashing out at anyone. Kit had never been big on make-up or dresses, or anything girly for that matter. But for Jessie, she'd do it all. She wanted to look pretty for him. No, not pretty. She wanted to look spectacular. So much so that he was rendered speechless when she walked down that aisle.

Barely dressed in her underwear and a robe, she exited the bathroom with a smile and excitement coursing through her blood. Today was the day she was getting married.

"So, my expert *Madrina de Matrimonia*, where to first?"

"The spa. You can eat some breakfast while you get your hair done, but you need to do the spa stuff first."

Kit tried not to laugh at Kelly's blush as they left her hotel room. For a thirteen year old, Kelly was mature for her age. Poor kid hadn't had a choice, having to grow up fast, but in some ways she was still an innocent young teenager. And apparently talking about waxing and body grooming was outside her comfort zone.

Jessie paced over the small wooden deck that had been set up on the beach. It was about six feet square and had tall timber poles on each corner. More timber poles lay atop the side poles and white gauzy material hung across to form a roof of sorts. There were red pieces in among the white and the chairs sitting to either side of the isle leading up to it had red sashes on their white coverings. The seats were already full. Jake, Sophie,

Dominic and Adele were all sitting, looking relaxed and happy. Jessie wasn't. He was beginning to worry. Kit was late.

"The bride is meant to be late, Jessie. Don't stress."

Pedro spoke up from where he stood near Gabriela, *la official* Jessie had found. She was fluent in English and had been happy to conduct the ceremony in the language. Kit knew a little Spanish, but not enough to smoothly speak her vows. All their Australian guests didn't speak a word of it, so it was easier to do it all in English.

"Relax, son. You know how Kit likes to sleep in. I bet she's been running late all day."

Jessie nodded at Jake after he called out. He was right. No-one would ever accuse Kit of being a morning person. He glanced up the beach for the hundredth time and his heart stopped beating for a moment before it started pounding double time. Choden in his red and yellow monk robe was easy to spot, as was Kelly in her scarlet sundress.

Kit, his sun, his moon and his stars, was walking toward him. Heaven help him, she was in a dress. Jessie grinned. He'd half expected her to turn up in pants. Maybe even bike leathers. He wouldn't put it past his soon-to-be wife.

Her dress was gorgeous. It was pure white, which contrasted brilliantly against her tanned skin and red hair. The strapless top of the gown molded to her breasts perfectly. There was a wide strip of shiny material around her waist. Satin maybe? Layers of sheer white lace in various lengths hung down from it to create the skirt. The front stopped over her knee and the back just touched the sand behind her. It was simple and delicate, and made Kit look like an elegant lady. Jessie had thought the green gown she'd worn at the rally gala dinner was amazing; this dress made that one look like rags.

Kit had one arm curled around Choden's and in the other hand she held a small bunch of flowers. Large white lilies, with what appeared to be small blue orchids. *Guess that's her something blue.* Her fiery red tresses had been left to tumble around her shoulders. The natural waves had been boosted into curls and a small chunk from each side had been pulled back from her face.

He didn't realize he was holding his breath until his lungs began to burn. As he took a great pull of air in, he could hear Pedro chuckling behind him.

"*Mi reinita.*"

He breathed the words as Kit and Choden came to stand before him. Kelly took the flowers from Kit as Choden took Jessie's hand and pressed Kit's palm against it. With a smile and a nod of his head, he silently moved away. Transfixed, Jessie stared into her precious face. She was so beautiful and about to be his wife. Already his mate, she was his forever.

With a sweet smile, Kit looked down and blushed a little before he led her the few steps to where Gabriela waited for them. Nerves had his heart beating fast and he tightened his grip on Kit's hand. She squeezed back as

Gabriela welcomed everyone and started the ceremony. Jessie wasn't really listening. He couldn't pull his focus away from Kit. Since they'd mated, he could feel her on a deeper level. So he knew, like him, she was nervous. He wanted to hold her. Kiss her until she melted against him and relaxed into bliss with him.

"Please face one another to exchange your vows."

With a little jerk, Jessie forced himself out of his thoughts as he turned to face Kit. Vows. He and Kit had written their own. They'd done it partly together so they were similar, but not quite the same. He didn't feel like they said enough but Kit had assured him they were perfect.

"I believe you've both prepared your own vows. Jessie?"

Jessie cleared his throat and wet his dry lips.

"Kit, *mi reinita*.

In your eyes, I have found my home.

In your heart, I have found my love.

In your soul, I have found my mate.

With you, I am whole, complete.

You make me laugh. You let me cry.

You are my breath, my every heartbeat.

I am yours.

You are mine.

Our hearts entwined,

As they forever will be."

Kit needed no prompting from Gabriela. With a sheen of tears in her eyes, which pulled at Jessie's heart, she spoke her vows to him.

"Jessie, *mi rey*.

I'm home when I'm by your side,

I'm grounded when I'm in your arms.

Under your care, I have found love.

In your soul, I have found my mate.

With you, I am whole, complete.

Through laughter and tears,

You are my rock, my every heartbeat.

I am yours.

You are mine.

Our hearts entwined,

As they forever will be."

Jessie felt a tear slip free from his eye but he didn't care. She'd called him her king in Spanish. She'd tweaked other parts since they'd sat down together to start writing them, and she blew him away with what she'd said. Somehow, he'd managed to find his perfect match.

"Who has the rings?"

Pedro moved forward and handed Gabriela their wedding rings. She handed him Kit's and he lifted Kit's hand in his.

"Kit, with this ring I promise to always be there for you. Your friend, your lover and your confidant. Whatever you need me to be, I'm yours eternally."

His voice had gone tight with emotion and a lump all but closed off his throat as he slid on the band of white gold and claimed Kit as his. Kit spoke the same words to him in a voice equally hoarse with emotion and as she slid his ring on, his heart lit up. Finally, she was his, just as he was hers.

"By the power vested in me, I now pronounce you husband and wife. You may kiss your bride."

Kit smiled so wide her cheeks hurt when Gabriela announced them husband and wife. *Jessie is officially all mine.* They were mated and married. Kit couldn't remember a time when she'd been happier. She gazed up into Jessie's silver-blue eyes, and he gave her a wolfish grin before he cupped her face with both palms and lowered his lips to hers. Expecting a light peck because they were the center of attention, she gasped a little in shock when he took her mouth in a passion filled kiss that made her toes curl. She gripped his waist and pressed herself against him as he ate at her mouth. The world faded away, and nothing existed aside from the two of them. His scent filled her senses and his warmth enveloped her. She would never get enough of her mate.

The sound of someone clearing his throat had Kit jerking from the kiss as embarrassment flared through her, heating her face. Cheers and laughter erupted around them and with a groan she buried her face against Jessie's throat. She knew she was blushing like a damn schoolgirl. She felt Jessie press a kiss to the top of her head before Pedro spoke quietly to Jessie.

"You've got paperwork to sign before you can get all snuggly, *amigo*."

Glad for the distraction, she straightened and Jessie took her hand in his as they went to a small table Gabriela had set up with the paperwork they needed to sign to make their marriage legal.

It didn't take long to complete all the formalities. Choden came forward to bless them in his native tongue with a Buddhist prayer. Even though Kit didn't know what exactly he'd said, Choden's tone was peaceful and loving. She blinked rapidly to stop tears falling. Neither she nor Jessie had any biological family here at their wedding, but having their leap family here supporting them helped ease the ache. Kit had given the twins all the information she could about her mother and she prayed Jordan and Joel could find her.

Choden gave them both a short hug before stepping back to allow the others a chance. Kit was grateful that Jessie kept his arm around her as everyone took their turn in congratulating them. A deep sense of contentment had spread through Kit, and she felt like she floated up the beach toward the hotel when they'd finished.

Kit was sitting next to Jessie in a private dining room surrounded by her leap family. They'd all finished eating and Kelly had convinced Dominic to dance with her. Kit smiled at how cute father and daughter looked playing around. The room was fairly large for their small group, and it had a smooth timber dance floor where Kelly and Dominic were currently goofing off. No doubt Kelly would drag them all out there at some point tonight.

Kit and Jessie had decided against having any kind of

formal reception. Jessie had agreed with her that they didn't need it. A cozy dinner with those who were closest to them was how they wanted to complete their special day.

After the dessert dishes were taken away, Jake approached her and silently slipped into Kelly's vacant seat beside her.

"I have a present from the twins for you, Kit."

She turned to Jake with a frown. "No presents, Jake. I told you—and them—that. The leap has given me more than I deserve already. I won't accept it."

He gave her a gentle smile as he took her hand in his. "Oh, I suspect you'll want this. It's some information you'll want to read."

Confused, Kit took the envelope Jake pressed into her palm and ripped it open. Inside was a small folded piece of paper. She pulled it free and began to read the short note. She knew by the masculine scribble that Jordan had written it.

Dear Kit,

Congratulations on your wedding. Sorry we couldn't join you in person, but we're there in spirit with you, big sister.

We've had success locating your mother. Since leaving Gabriel, Camila remarried and currently lives with her husband and two sons on the mainland. They have a secluded farm near Parnkas Point, which is near the Coorong in South Australia. They were tricky to find. Joel is certain she went as much off grid as she could to stay hidden from Gabriel.

Enjoy your wedding night and we'll see you soon, big sister.

Love Jordan and Joel.

Tears streamed down her face and she covered her mouth with her hand. They'd found her mother!

Jessie's strong arm came around her shoulders and pulled her in against his side.

"Kit? Are you okay? What's wrong?"

She turned to look into Jessie's eyes. "They actually found her. The twins have found my mother."

Noticing the room had gone quiet, she turned to see everyone looking at her. Did they all know? She sought out Dominic and as soon as she caught his gaze he started toward her.

"We know. The twins told me and Dad a few days ago and we thought it would make a nice wedding gift. They agreed. I've spoken with Xander and as soon as your team has finished in Hobart, you'll be going to South Australia to both find your mother and start the search."

Gratitude and hope overwhelmed Kit.

"Thank you, Dominic."

She sprung from her seat to embrace her leap brother and he held her close.

"You are most welcome, little sister."

Dominic released her, and she felt Jessie wrap his arms around her waist from behind.

"Looks like next year is going to be another busy one, hey Dominic?"

Dominic groaned as he rubbed his face with his hand. "Well, it will be doing well to top this last one."

Kit smirked over at him. "Dominic, you really should know better than to tempt fate like that."

Other Fire and Snow books:

Coming Soon:

The next instalment of Fire and Snow is Fierce Guardian, which tells Xander and Rachel's journey.

Out Now:

Guardian's Heart
Fire and Snow: Book One

The last thing Snow Leopard Shifter Dominic expects to find at an accident scene is his mate, the beautiful Adele. But after four years of dreaming of her, there she is, right in front of him. However, winning the heart of his lonely, grieving mate is no simple task. Just as their relationship begins to heat up, a gravely injured child, Kelly, stumbles into their lives after escaping and fleeing her abuser. Will Dominic and Adele's bond grow stronger as they nurture and protect Kelly? Will their relationship be able to survive all that fate plans on throwing their way?

Noble Guardian
Fire and Snow: Book Two

After watching his older brother win the heart of his mate, Conner White can't wait for his turn. When he finally has his first dream of his mate, he is both relieved that he knows who she is and worried as he hasn't been able to get near her since he caught a glimpse of her at his brother's wedding weeks earlier.

Tina Anderson is beyond miserable. Her mother abandoned her after a life altering injury that left the vibrant gymnast in a wheelchair. Her father has been forced to leave her to go work off shore. She's been left in the care of a harsh bitter woman who is only after her father and will do whatever she deems necessary to take her place in his life. No matter the cost.

Conner and Tina's road to happiness is filled with twists, turns and pot holes, but are they strong enough to pull each other through it all?

276

www.ingramcontent.com/pod-product-compliance
Lightning Source LLC
Chambersburg PA
CBHW061020120726
47910CB00006B/2025